THE HERETICS SERIES BOOK 2

THE SERPENT AND THE DOVE

By Glen Robinson

Prevail Publications

Prevail Publications
321 CR 805A
Cleburne, TX 76031

Except for God, of course, all characters, names, corporations, institutions, organizations, events, or locales in this novel are a product of the author's overworked imaginations or, if real, used fictitiously. Any resemblance to real people, places, or things, living or dead, is a product of yours.

Heretic Series, Volume 2, First Edition

Cover Design by Hell Yes Designs, https://www.hellyes.design

TABLE OF CONTENTS

Acknowledgements

A sincere thank you to Dennis & Irma Balazs, Ben Torres and Thea Plosceanu, for checking the translation of the Hungarian, Spanish and Romanian text here, respectively.

Thanks to the Rough Writers Creative Writing Club for their critique and support during the writing of this book.

"And we know that in all things God words for the good of those who love him, who have been called according to his purpose." –Romans 8:28

"Whenever Christ calls us, his call leads us to death."
  –Dietrich Bonhoeffer

1

Oil's Well That Ends Well

New Orleans
Sometime before midnight
Dec. 31

It was dark, and Holly was terrified.

The past few hours had been a nightmarish blur. It started with a whirlwind trip with friends through the bars and clubs in the French Quarter, where it seemed the entire world was eager to celebrate the turn of the new year. Then she had met some cute guys and shared some flirty conversation and suddenly found herself blacking out. The next thing she knew, she was here, wherever here was. Holly's hands were bound behind her, a bag was over her head, and she could hear the sobbing of other girls in the darkness around her. Holly was frightened by what was happening to her, but as she realized that others were suffering the same fate, she knew that this was a lot bigger deal that just one person. She took a minute to take deep breaths and tried to calm herself, reminding herself that panic would solve nothing. Then she tried to analyze her situation.

She was lying on some rough wooden planks, and she suspected that she was in an attic or a basement, based on the musty smell that surrounded her. It was either that or it was the bag over her head that contributed to that smell, she reasoned. In any case, she tried to calm herself.

And then she heard heavy footsteps above her. *So, it's a basement,* she thought. The steps weren't that far above her head, so the space couldn't be that large. It was, however, large enough for the other girls that she heard crying there, at least three of them as far as she could tell.

The footsteps approached and a door opened, most likely a trapdoor. Despite the bag over her head, she saw blurry light filter through from above. Two figures were standing there. One approached, and she realized they were adding another girl to the basement. *Poor girl*, Holly thought. The girl's body thudded down onto the beams next to her, and the door slammed shut above them.

"It's all right," Holly hissed. "You're going to be okay."

There was a pause, then the other girl whispered back hoarsely. "Of course, we are. What's your name?"

Holly raised an eyebrow under her bag. "My name is Holly. I'm from Detroit."

"Well, Holly from Detroit. I'm Taupe from Austin. And we're going to get out of here."

Holly took a breath and held it. "You sound pretty sure of yourself. I wish I had your confidence."

Taupe chuckled. "Well Holly, do you believe in God? Do you pray?"

Holly bit her lip. "I've been praying since I got here."

"Well, yes, I'm pretty sure of myself. First, because I believe God answers our prayers. And second, I also believe in helping others who need help. And finally...."

"Yes?" Holly said.

Taupe responded by pulling the hood off Holly's head. Holly looked up at Taupe, who was smiling. In the light streaming through the cracks in the beams above them, Holly could see that Taupe was a muscular, attractive black woman in her mid-20s. Holly smiled back.

"I've been practicing getting zip ties off for several weeks now," Taupe said. "These were a cinch. Let's get your arms free and then we'll get your friends loose."

"What about the men upstairs? I'm pretty sure they have guns."

Taupe grinned in the gloom of the sub-basement. "I have friends of my own."

* * *

Port of New Orleans
Jan. 1, Midnight

From his vantage point on the top of the building outside the barbed-wire enclosure, gray-haired Harris Borden sat behind bags of sand listening to the fireworks popping in the distance over the tourist areas of the French Quarter in New Orleans. He could almost hear the countdown of "three, two, one" and then "Happy New Year!" shouted through the air by the thousands who were celebrating the new calendar year. With the bunch that he was now connected with, there was a time when he might have even had heard that chatter in the comms back and forth, as undisciplined as it was.

Not anymore. Taupe. Josh. Peewee. Rojo. Bobby. He shook his head in disbelief, amazed that he was able to pull the entire team back together again, and they seemed better than ever. Bobby was still in his wheelchair but situated in his dependable RV command center just a half block away, his half a dozen drones hovering in strategic locations around the stockade. Harris looked down at the tablet in front of him and could see all six viewpoints, showing armed guards either distracted by the fireworks or half asleep at their posts.

Taupe had been successful in being picked up by the kidnappers, and they had followed her and her captors back to the warehouse. The drones had recorded every step as the kidnappers had forced her from the van, bound and gagged, into the warehouse, just fifteen minutes before. Harris and his team hadn't even needed to activate the tracer they had embedded under her skin.

He nodded to himself. "Action," Harris said into his comms.

Like shadows in the night, three black figures moved silently across the tarmac toward the warehouse.

* * *

Austin, Texas
The Home of Ruth and Douglas Washington

3

"So, explain to me again why we are here, hundreds of miles away, while the old guys get to have all the fun?" Connie said to Ruth. The young college sophomore sat on the couch in Ruth's living room, with mid-30s Ruth sitting on a chair nearest the large flatscreen TV, a headset on her head. Adam, her on-again, off-again boyfriend, sat on the other end of the couch, eating popcorn.

"Consider yourself fortunate," Ruth said. "We didn't have this kind of technology when we went through training. You're going to learn from the pros. And, because this is happening live, you get to share any mistakes as they happen as well."

"I seem to recall that you were one of the best," Connie said. She picked up a photo in a frame on the end table that showed a young Ruth standing with her brother Josh and Harris Borden in San Francisco. Neither Ruth nor Josh looked like they were more than sixteen years old, and both looked like they were probably homeless. "Why is it that you're stuck back here with the children instead of out there on the front line?"

"Someone had to be here with you."

Adam cleared his throat. "That's not what I heard. I heard that this assignment was too much like one where some people got killed when you were in charge. They decided to leave you behind for your own good." He caught Connie giving him an evil stare. "What? It's true, isn't it?"

Ruth shook her head. "That happened a long time ago. And it was on a ship, not a warehouse. In any case, you two are missing what's happening. Let's pay attention, students."

"Yes, ma'am," Connie said. They turned back to the screen.

* * *

Josh led the assault team on the ground. It had been a while, and Taupe had argued that she would be a better fit for that assignment. But it was obvious that she would be needed to learn where the girls were being kept. They had trained for this assignment for four weeks, and Josh had worked out non-stop, making sure that he was up for the job. He not only wanted to make sure that he didn't disappoint Harris on this assignment. He wanted to make sure that the team came through unscathed.

As it was, the assault was timed perfectly. The fireworks going off in the sky were a great distraction, and with their dark clothes and blackened faces, they got within arm's reach of the outside guards before they were seen. As the guard nearest Josh turned in alarm to confront him, Josh shot him with his taser point blank. The guard shook violently, then with Josh's assistance, fell silently to the ground.

"Splash one," Josh whispered, and heard responses on the comms from the other two as they took out their guards.

"Infrared says four actives inside," Josh heard Bobby say from his RV command center. "You boys gonna be okay?"

"Think you could stir up a diversion on the south side?" Josh asked after they had zip-tied the three guards.

Josh heard Bobby chuckle. "It will be my pleasure."

A long moment later, Josh heard small explosions on the opposite side of the warehouse. Josh saw the hulking shape of a Samoan and a smaller Mexican-American in the darkness and waved for Peewee and Rojo to join him. The three of them entered the big building and saw that most of it was abandoned and empty, but one small area had a table and chairs, some sleeping bags and cots and an ice chest with a small camping stove on top.

"Looks like they've been camped out here for a while," Peewee whispered.

"You two go find the girls and get them out of here," Josh said. "I will keep the bad guys occupied for a few minutes. But be quick about it."

Josh went in search of the kidnappers. He found all four of them on the far side of the warehouse. He crouched behind some metal shelving and watched them. The explosions—what sounded to Josh like cherry bombs popping—continued as he approached the four men, and Josh grinned, then frowned. He wondered how long Bobby's drones would be able to distract the men, and how long it would be before they realized that they were in no danger.

"Come on," one of them, who looked like the leader, said. "It's just fireworks or something. I don't see anyone out there. We need to keep an eye on the merchandise."

The leader turned and started to head back toward their small camp when Josh took a can of synthetic motor oil from the shelf beside him and threw it into the darkness behind them.

"What was that?" an exceptionally large man with an AK-47 asked. "That weren't no fireworks."

"No, it wasn't," the leader said. He reached down to his belt and pulled out a pistol, then reached for a small radio. "Radio check, Charlie one," he said. "How you guys doing out there?" He waited for a long moment, but there was no answer. And Josh knew there wouldn't be one since they had taken out the guards at the entrances.

"You," the leader pointed to the larger man with the AK-47. "Go check that out." He pointed to the darkness. "The rest of you come with me. Something's wrong here."

In the meantime, Josh had taken two more cans of synthetic motor oil and loosened the lids on the cans. As the three of them started back the way they had come, Josh threw one, then the other can in quick succession. The first can hit the leader in the chest and knocked him over, with the oil splashing all over him. The second can hit the ground and covered the concrete floor, making it difficult to stand.

The three men slipped and slid, trying to get their footing, while the fourth had already left to find out what was happening in the darkness where the first can had been thrown.

"Boris!" the leader shouted. "Get back here!" The big man returned. The leader gestured at the dark shelving where Josh had been standing. In response, the man raised his automatic rifle and began firing wildly in Josh's direction.

Josh beat a hasty retreat. He didn't know if they would come looking for him or forget him and go back to the kidnapped girls, but he knew that he needed to get between them and the team that was trying to rescue the girls.

"Progress report?" Josh hissed into his comms set. He was making a wide circle and heading back toward them.

"We're working on it," Rojo said. "Found the trap door, but it's bolted and padlocked. And tasers don't do much against padlocks."

"You two don't know how to pick locks?" Bobby said.

"Never learned."

"Find a metal pry bar and break it," Josh said. "Hurry, these guys are getting wise to my bag of tricks."

"Got it, boss," Rojo said. "Just need a couple more minutes."

Yeah, right. Josh frowned and looked around him on the darkened shelves that surrounded him. *Lord, give me inspiration,* he prayed.

Josh looked around him and saw a variety of automobile parts boxed and stacked on the shelves: batteries, alternators, tires, steering wheels. He decided to climb up on top of one of the metal shelves that rose ten feet up on either side of him and see if he could see where the kidnappers were. He climbed up quickly and saw that they were only two aisles away, still trying to wipe off the oil that covered them. The two others had joined the leader in drawing automatic pistols, while the man with the rifle had disappeared. Josh realized that he needed to keep them together.

There was a four-inch cast-iron pipe used for the sprinkler system running about three feet above the top of the shelf that Josh was standing on. The shelves didn't appear to be anchored down by anything other than their own weight, which gave Josh an idea. He gripped the pipe above him and put his feet against the edge of the shelf he was standing on, pushing it sideways. It was very heavy, and at first, he didn't think he could budge it. But he continued to push, and after a long moment, he felt it groan and the whole shelf began to lean away from him. He strained and then he felt it give.

The whole shelf, perhaps thirty feet in length, filled with tires and batteries, tipped over and collapsed with a roar. As he watched, he could see the three men on the other side of the second aisle look up in horror at the avalanche of automobile parts that came crashing down on them. Josh watched as the shelf he was on collapsed, as well as the one next to it, trapping the three men on the other side. The noise from the crash was deafening.

He hung from the pipe on the ceiling thirteen feet above the floor for several seconds, trying to decide what to do. Then he dropped to the floor, wincing as his knees absorbed the fall.

"Status report," he said to his comm, standing up to brush himself off. He was rewarded by the barrel of an automatic rifle stuck in his face.

"I got your status report right here," he heard beside him. It was the big man who had disappeared into the darkness earlier. "On your knees. I'll make this quick."

Josh didn't have a chance to respond to him, or even get down on his knees. Out of nowhere, what looked like a broom handle appeared and whacked the big man across the temple. Then it hit him several more times. Josh turned and saw the man collapse to the ground, just as Taupe appeared out of the darkness.

"Aren't we supposed to be rescuing *you*?" Josh said to the tall Black woman.

Taupe grinned and tipped her head. "I got bored. The girls are fine, since you asked."

"So I suppose Peewee and Rojo found a way to pry the door open?"

"Something like that. Feds are here."

Josh frowned. "Aw, now you had to go and spoil it. We have to spend the next few hours answering questions."

Taupe laughed. "As I recall, you and the Feds go way back. You should be fine." She looked down at the man at her feet, then over at the collapsed shelving. "What about these guys?"

Josh shrugged. "Let the Feds take care of them."

* * *

The home of Douglas and Ruth Washington
Austin, Texas
Later That Day

"So that's got to be a first," Bobby said, laughing. "Josh taking down bad guys using tires and batteries."

They were all enjoying down time after the rescue. Some were sitting in the expansive living room on the couch and chairs, while others were getting pizza, fruit salad, tacos, chips and other refreshments in the connected dining room. A pool table was set up in the family room on the other side, where Adam and Peewee were playing and a few watched.

"Then hanging from the ceiling like an orangutan, no less," Josh added. He shook his head.

"And all six young women were rescued and appear to be fine," Ruth said. "They will probably need some counseling, but that's to be expected."

"I'm just grateful no one got hurt," Taupe said. "None of you guys, at least."

"Actually, not even the kidnappers got hurt," Josh said. "Not really. And that's good."

"Why?" Connie said. "Why is that good?" She spoke from the living room couch, where she sat nibbling on a plate heaped with fruit salad.

Josh smiled slightly. "They needed to be stopped and arrested. But we didn't want them hurt, not really. There's no reason for that. Just because they're in the business of hurting people doesn't mean we have to be as well."

"Explain to me again why this whole thing wasn't turned over to the New Orleans Police?" Connie asked, her eyebrow raised. Josh chuckled and he turned to Harris.

"I'm going to defer to Harris on this one," Josh said.

Harris Borden sat quietly looking out the window at the afternoon light. He turned when it got quiet, and he heard his name.

9

"What was that?" he said.

"The question was, why did we perform the rescue instead of turning it over to the police?" a voice repeated. It came from the room where Adam and Peewee were playing pool, and Connie recognized it was from Douglas Washington, former congressman, adjunct professor of history and husband of Ruth. Douglas stepped into the room with the others. "I've wondered that question myself for a while." The room grew quiet, and Harris looked at Douglas, then turned to Connie.

"There are some things we'd like to turn over to the police," Harris responded. "And we do. When we have enough to get them involved, it's a lot cleaner that way. We don't rub the locals the wrong way, and crime in the area doesn't get wise to what we're doing. But there are times when it's not smart."

"Such as?" Douglas said.

"Such as when the local police are notorious for taking bribes from the people accused of being involved in the crime," Taupe said, speaking up. "I've seen it too many times. We turn in names and nothing happens. Or worse, the people we are trying to protect catch the bad end of things."

"And there are times when we don't have enough legal evidence for police to act," Harris said. "Such as last night. We had to catch them in the act. That's why we used Taupe. We called in the Feds when we knew everyone was safe and the bad guys were not going to run. That's how we do things."

Douglas cleared his throat. "You're forgetting a couple of things, Harris. First, we have a system in place to take care of this. Due process. When we amateurs take it upon ourselves to enforce the law, it makes it harder for law enforcement to do their jobs. And second, sooner or later, one of us is going to get killed doing this."

"Douglas, Douglas," Ruth said quietly behind him. She stepped forward and put her arms on his shoulders. "You're not a congressman anymore. Step down from your bully pulpit and let's just enjoy the moment."

There was an awkward silence while Harris and Douglas stared at each other across the room. Suddenly, Adam broke the quiet from the other room.

"Hey, Prof. Washington," Adam said. "Time for me to kick your butt at pool. Or are you up for it?"

Douglas nodded slowly, still staring at Harris. "I'll be right there."

Connie watched as Douglas went slowly into the other room to play pool. A moment later, Harris' cell phone buzzed, and he looked at it. He stood up and went through the double glass doors out onto the patio overlooking the river, closing the door behind him. A moment later, he was into a serious conversation.

"What's with those two?" Connie said quietly to Taupe, who sat across from her. "I thought everyone in the Heretics were friends."

Taupe shrugged. "Time changes things, I guess. Harris has his way of doing things, and Douglas has been known to challenge the status quo now and again. He's not always easy to be around. Ask Ruth."

She gestured at Douglas' wife, who stood at the edge of the room where Douglas played pool. As she watched her, Connie realized that Ruth seemed to be torn between two worlds: the political world of her husband and the mysterious, spiritual world of Harris Borden.

"What's with you and Adam?" Taupe whispered back to Connie. "Not getting along?"

Connie shrugged. "We're taking a break. He got tired of my drama trying to get through training and I got tired of the drama of seeing him flirting with other girls. We agreed to disagree. Still friends though."

"Too bad," Taupe said. "You two were a cute couple."

"Yeah, well," Connie said, watching Adam playing pool in the other room. "Life, or something like it, goes on."

* * *

Ruth Washington was happy to have everyone over to their home overlooking Lake Travis, especially on such a crisp, clear New Year's

Day. It seemed like forever since this many of the old guard had come together, and even with many now situated in Austin, it was rare that the team got together for social events. Even so, she nervously watched both her husband Douglas and Harris Borden after the unusual confrontation that had just happened.

She watched Harris outside on the deck. He was just finishing the phone call, and his face looked very serious. He switched off the phone and looked off into the distance, and she took that as her cue to go out and join him. He turned slightly when the door opened, and she stepped out onto the deck.

"One of the perks of living in Texas," Ruth said as she walked up to Harris. "I never thought I'd be walking out on my deck in shirt sleeves on New Year's Eve, overlooking a view like that."

"Back home in St. Petersburg, we're entering our third month of winter," Harris said, smiling slightly. "The snow is probably two feet deep right now."

"Is that who was calling?"

Harris shook his head. "No, since Katya died last spring, and Harris Jr. decided to go his own way, I've not had a lot of calls from Mother Russia." He sighed and looked sadly at Ruth.

"It wasn't your fault, you know," Ruth said. "You were in prison. You couldn't have done anything about her. And if you could have helped with the cancer, you would. You tried."

Harris nodded. He looked back at the group inside the house.

"Quite a show we put on in there," Harris said quietly.

Ruth smiled slightly. "A lot is going on with Douglas. He's under a lot of pressure. People in high places want him to do things he's not sure about. It makes him question things." She looked at Harris. "Can you find an opportunity to talk to him? He always respected you."

Harris raised an eyebrow. "Sounded in there like he was ready to challenge me, more likely. But yes, I'll look for an opportunity to talk to him."

"There's something else, Harris," Ruth said. "Taupe wanted to talk to you, but as the person in charge of training I thought it was my responsibility. She's worried about Connie."

"What about Connie?" Harris looked back into the room where Connie sat on the couch listening to others tell their stories of past exploits of the Heretics. "She's a brilliant girl, Ruth," Harris said. "She's going to have some rough edges."

"It's not that," Ruth said. "Her psychological and mental preparation are stellar. In fact, she's the top of the class. Of course, with her and Adam, we only have two in the class, so far."

"Go on."

"It's her physical training that Taupe is worried about. She's a klutz. Two left feet. Taupe has tried and tried to teach her basic gymnastics, self-defense moves, even just balance techniques. No luck."

"How bad is it?" Harris asked.

"Bad enough that I'm afraid to send her out on any missions," Ruth said. "If she doesn't hurt herself, she's almost guaranteed to get a team member killed. Couple that with the fact that she has a family in Dallas, and I don't see how she ever got this far."

Harris nodded. "I see. That's a lot to think about. Let me digest that."

"So…what *was* the phone call about?"

"Well, I'm not sure how what you just said fits with my call, but it appears that our world is about to change."

"Change? How?"

"That call was from a pastor friend of mine in Japan. The Heretics are about to go international. I'm about to take a little trip, and considering our conversation, it might be a good idea to invite your husband along." **γ**

2

Veritas

Eilean Donan, Scotland
New Year's Day

The fog was slowly burning off the three lochs outside the world-famous castle known as Eilean Donan, one of the most iconic images in Scotland. Visitors normally would be flocking to the site to enjoy the view of the castle on an island first built in the mid-13th Century. But with the winter's bite, and the "closed for renovation" signs that blocked the bridge to the island that held the castle, no tourists were around. Instead, Eilean Donan was reserved for sole use by a handful of billionaires formerly known as the Brotherhood of the Altar, but lately referred to as the Consortium.

"Blast this cold," Ian Target said, rubbing his hands together and standing by a fireplace tall enough to walk into without stooping and eight feet across. Despite his complaints, the fire inside roared, and a member of the waitstaff brought him another hot toddy.

"Come, drink your hot rum and join us," McArthur Henson said to Target, gesturing to him from a massive mahogany table that dominated the room. The walls were covered with tapestries and shields, armor, and swords. Leaded glass in vaulted windows high above them let the light pour in. Rich red and blue carpets covered the thick wooden plank floors. But this group was oblivious to all of it. Instead, they were more fixated in current events that affected them all.

"A drop in the bucket, I tell you," McArthur Henson was telling the man next to him at the table. He flicked cigar ashes on the large mahogany table as he talked. "Sure, they interrupted your plans in New Orleans. But you're only talking about six young women. Six! Bother me when the number is six hundred."

"You don't get it," Sergio Estevez said, shaking his head. "This isn't a one-time problem. They're a chronic problem. These *comejenes* have been around for years. And I for one want them gone."

"Sergio is right," Ian Target said as he put his drink down on the table. "In fact, that's why I joined this consortium. I'm rich, and I used to think I had the resources to do whatever I wanted or needed to do in the world. I hired mercenaries, very good ones, but apparently that wasn't enough. These *comejenes*, as you put them, have been an irritant to me and to a lot of people for a long time. So, what are we going to about these Heretics?"

"We have dossiers on these people that go back to the beginning," Cullen Stone said as he entered the room from the massive double doors leading out to the hallway. "Our organization likes to stay private, which requires us to work in the shadows. But that doesn't mean we can't gather information. In fact, our investigative resources rival the CIA and Russian intelligence. But we need to think seriously about our next step."

"I believe Harris Borden has decided that for us," Ian Target said. "My sources tell me that he's joined forces with a coalition of Christian leaders intent on turning the Heretics into an international organization." He paused and looked out over the table at the other billionaires there. "If that happens, our minor irritant will no longer be minor."

"*Sangre y cenizas,*" muttered Estevez, and others swore under their breath as well.

"Calm down, calm down," Cullen Stone said. "This consortium has been around for almost six hundred years, and a small group of *Christians*"—he spat the word out—"is not going to stop our plans now or anytime in the future. We have contingencies for this sort of thing. Mr. Target, I already knew about this contact between Harris Borden and the coalition. In fact, my sources tell me three teams are being sent to America for training. We'll need to take care of them. Austin may still be a bit too high profile at present, but our hands aren't completely tied."

As he spoke, the big oaken doors opened behind him. Surprised, Cullen Stone turned to see a man in his fifties being accompanied by their head of security.

"Who is this?" Stone barked. "You know that we are not to be disturbed. Why did you let him in?"

"My apologies, sir," the head of security said. "But this man needs to be here." He turned and looked at the man with a strange reverence in his face. He then turned and left, closing the door behind him.

"Who in blazes are you?" Stone barked at the man. The newcomer was slight of build, about five foot eight, with dark hair and an unassuming face. He was dressed in a tweed jacket and casual slacks. He could have gone unnoticed in any crowd. He smiled at Cullen Stone, then at the rest of the men.

"Who am I? Well, that's an important question, isn't it? I've gone by many different names over the years, but you can call me Veritas. Truth. Because I am here to bring truth to you."

"What are you talking about?" Ian Target said. He noticed a sweet aroma beginning to fill the room. "And what is that stench?"

"That, my friends, is the smell of power. Here I am, looking at eight of the most powerful men in the world. All of you billionaires. Raised to believe that the secret to power in this world is money. You control others by controlling the almighty dollar, or euro, as you prefer. But I am here to bring you the new truth. Money is not the source of power. Oh, no, my friends."

The sweet aroma had become overpowering in the room, turning from a sweet fragrance to a sickly, syrupy stench. A few of the men began to cough.

"Someone...someone needs to...." Cullen Stone began to say, but he never finished his sentence. He sat down abruptly and stared ahead of him into nothingness.

"So who wants to ask me what the ultimate source of power is?" He looked around the table at the men. Many had become white-faced, and one or two had pulled out handkerchiefs to wipe their brow. "You?" He pointed at Sergio Estevez. "Well, since many of you look like you're indisposed, I will tell you. It's about belief. Control what a person believes, and you control their actions. It's the ultimate power." He laughed and raised his hands as if to signal the completion of his speech. Quickly the aroma dissipated from the room.

The men sitting around the room blinked as if just waking up from a long nap. They stared at Veritas as if seeing him for the first time. Finally, Cullen Stone spoke, his eyes finding focus again.

"Yes. Yes, of course. I...I can't remember the last time someone made more sense in this consortium," he said, a note of reverence in his voice. "I am sure I speak for all of us when I say that we would be honored if you agreed to lead this group. Further, all the resources we have here, which are quite extensive, are at your disposal." Cullen Stone's voice, which had been strained at the beginning, became more relaxed as he accepted their fate.

Veritas looked at Cullen Stone, then at each of the eight men around the table and nodded.

"Thank you, gentlemen," he said simply. "I wouldn't have it any other way." He turned and looked out the window at the jaw-dropping view of the lochs outside their castle getaway.

"It's a beautiful place where you gentlemen have chosen to gather," Veritas said. "But I trust that this is a temporary retreat. I have big plans for your organization—*our* organization. And they won't be done from here. Tell me, what were you discussing before I came into the room?"

The room of billionaires looked at each other, then turned to look at Ian Target, who sat at the far end of the table.

"There is a small group of Christian zealots called the Heretics who have interfered in our plans too many times," Target said. "I recently sent mercenaries after them in Austin, Texas and these Heretics somehow escaped my attacks. In fact, they turned the tables on me, and I lost my yacht!"

"Ooh, he lost his yacht," Veritas mimicked Ian Target, then chuckled. "Sorry, but you were such an easy...*Target!* Get it? Don't worry, my brother. We will take care of them."

"The new development that we need to add is that the Heretics have been asked to expand and make their group international," Cullen Stone added quietly. "We were just about to deal with them."

"Of course, of course," Veritas said. "We should deal with the new teams first. Then since your approach with the Heretics in Austin has not worked so far, let me try my method."

The table of billionaires, used to getting their own way, sat quietly and agreed with their new leader, unsure as to what was going to happen next, but confident in Veritas.

* * *

In the Home of Douglas and Ruth Washington
Austin, Texas

Harris Borden got Ruth to help him gather everyone into the living room for the official announcement.

"Wow, would you look at us," Ruth said quietly. "This is really the largest number of Heretics-related people we've had in one place since…" She looked at the people who had either been involved in the rescue or had learned from it.

"Since San Pedro Harbor fifteen years ago," Harris said. "I wish I could have been there. Maybe things would have turned out differently. But this time, I have good news to share."

The others looked at him expectantly.

"That call was from Ito Tamaguchi, a young pastor in Japan. I went to seminary with his father. Apparently, Ito belongs to an international coalition of Christians who think the way we do. Somehow, they have heard about the Heretics.

"In our conversation, we agreed to do two things. First, I'm going to travel in a few days to Austria to meet with this coalition and explain our philosophy to the group and work out a plan for an international network of Heretic teams around the world." He turned and looked at Douglas. "D.J., I'd like for you to accompany me on this trip."

"Why me?" Douglas asked.

"I think you will provide some credibility as someone who has been a member of the United States Congress as well as some insights," Harris said. "Plus, I think you might learn a thing or two." His eyes twinkled as Douglas nodded in agreement.

"Second, at the same time, three teams will be arriving here by Friday to begin training. One is from South America, the second is from Asia, and the third is from the Middle East."

The group gasped and looked at each other. Harris grinned.

"Don't worry," he added. "They're all fluent in English."

"This is incredible," Taupe said. "And so unexpected."

"There's so much to do!" Josh said. "Can we be ready in time?"

"I have the utmost faith in you," Harris said, smiling.

* * *

Carothers Residence Hall,
University of Texas, Austin
A few days later

The chains on Connie's arms were thick and rusty, with links large enough for her to pass her fingers through. She looked around herself and realized that she recognized this place. It was the dungeon where she and two other girls had been held captive for close to a week after witches kidnapped them. In real life, they had been rescued by Ezra Huddleston, Connie's sister's boyfriend, just before they had been offered as human sacrifices. But now she was back here in this place.

Her mouth went dry, her throat threatening to close. She wanted to scream, but no sound came from her mouth. Finally, she thought to pray.

"Help me, Lord," she prayed, and the chains on her wrists went limp. She pulled on them and the links pulled apart. She pulled again, and the chains fell off her arms completely and to the floor.

"Hurry," she heard behind her. It was Ezra, beckoning for her to run. "We have to run. Hurry, Connie!"

"Connie, help me," she heard and looked back the other way. Still chained in the corner was her old friend Marita. She had been kidnapped just before Connie.

Now she had chains wrapped around her ankles and wrists. "Connie, don't leave me here!" she begged.

"Connie, we have to hurry!" Ezra shouted behind her. "They're coming!"

"I have to help Marita!" Connie said to Ezra. "I have to save her!" She turned and Ezra was gone. The room was filling with water, the stone steps rapidly covering with coldness.

"Connie, don't leave me!" she heard again, and turned to look for Marita. But Marita was no longer there. Instead, she heard footsteps coming down the stairs toward her. Time to run.

Connie woke up from her nightmare, her face and bedclothes drenched in sweat. She sat up and stared into the darkness for a long moment, trying to get her heart to stop racing. On the other side of the room, Dora, her Albanian roommate, was blissfully snoring away.

Was this just a dream, one of those you can chalk up to a bad piece of cheesecake? Or was this something more? She had heard stories from others in the Heretics about how God had tried to speak to them using dreams. Occasionally, someone would be visited by an angel, but Connie didn't get her hopes up that that would happen to her. But could God have been telling her something about Marita?

After everything that had happened, after the insanity in the dungeon, after the rescue and even after the trial, Marita had decided to go back to the coven. Connie shook her head in disbelief even now about it. Why would someone turn their back on proof that something wasn't good for them and choose it over a better path? Connie had tried to talk to her about it once, and Marita had warned Connie of her "Christian prejudice" and that it wasn't allowing her to see things as they really were. When Connie had said that she would pray for her, Marita had replied, "please don't."

Now Connie saw Marita on campus once in a while, and with classes beginning today, there was every possibility in the world that they would see each other more. Connie bowed her head and prayed.

"Lord, if this is you telling me that I need to help Marita, even after she told me to get lost, I understand. I will do my best. But please help me out a little bit, if you will. Let us cross paths somehow? Thanks."

She saw that it was still several hours till her alarm would ring, so she lay back down and tried to sleep.

Connie often had a hard time remembering her dreams, and she worried that she would forget this one as well. But when her alarm went off at 6:30 a.m., it was fresh in her mind. She did her devotions, took her shower, and got cleaned up and went over to the cafeteria for some breakfast. Her first class was at 8:30 and was one that she was really looking forward to: calligraphy. A gifted polyglot like her sister and her father, Connie had studied and mastered twelve languages, now including Mandarin, and was working on ten more. But to truly understand a language, it was best to understand the culture of the people who spoke that language, and much of the Chinese culture was wrapped up in calligraphy. That's why Connie had finally worked the Calligraphy class into her schedule, despite it being just another elective class among many that she had taken in the past two years.

"One of these days, I have to really get serious about a major," she muttered to herself. "Mom and Dad are going to expect me to graduate, and I don't think being a professional student is an option." Like her sister, Connie had started off as a linguistics major, which she could have easily completed since she knew so many languages. But she quickly lost interest, and for a while pursued journalism, following in the footsteps of Ezra Huddleston and even spent time in an internship recently at the local newspaper. But the opportunities there seemed limited, and so she soon lost interest there as well.

"God will provide," she muttered to herself, more as reassurance than anything, as she climbed the steps to the Doty Fine Arts Building and entered Room 111 where Mrs. Brinkmeyer was about to teach the first Calligraphy class. Connie paused as she came in the doorway and scanned the room for an empty seat. To her surprise, there was an empty seat in the back row, and it was next to Marita.

God will definitely provide, Connie thought to herself. That dream she had the night before had to be directed at her. God was telling her that she needed to help her friend. And He was making it as easy as He could.

Marita was checking out the supplies for the class that were laid out on the large desk in front of her and didn't look up as Connie stepped up to her. Connie smiled and spoke up.

"Hi, Marita," Connie said. "Looks like we had the same idea."

Marita looked up in surprise when she saw Connie there. Connie saw a mixture of emotions cross her face: first shock, then joy, then fear. Suddenly a defensive wall went up and Marita's face clouded.

"I don't think this is a good idea," she muttered. She stood up and gathered her things, moving to a seat two rows forward. She didn't look at Connie as she did so.

"What do I do now, Lord?" Connie whispered to herself. "Do I go after her?"

But Connie decided to wait and see, her heart heavy in her chest.

3

The Serpent and the Dove

Bergstrom International Airport
Austin, Texas

Ruth dropped Harris and Douglas off at the airport and they went straight toward check-in. Harris went through the front desk, followed by Douglas, and then they headed toward the security checkpoint, where they stood in line to be processed.

"Let me take a look at that," Douglas said, reaching for Harris' Russian passport. "How did you manage to get your citizenship switched over to Russian?"

Harris shrugged. "I've got dual citizenship. With me spending so much time in Russia and my past history, it's easier this way."

Douglas flipped through it. "I'll have to admit, it's prettier than the U.S. passport."

"What was the holdup at check in?"

Douglas shrugged. "I had to let them know that I had a weapon packed in my luggage."

Harris' eyebrows raised. "You brought a *weapon*? What kind?"

"Just an automatic pistol. I always carry one."

Harris clucked his tongue. "They won't let you carry that in a foreign country, you know. Austria's pretty strict about those kinds of things."

Douglas smiled slightly. "They won't complain if they don't know about it. Besides, we might need it." They came up to the security officer and stopped their conversation. They went through the scanning equipment. When they got to the other side, Harris frowned and approached Douglas again.

"Since when do the Heretics carry guns?" Harris hissed. He looked around him at the others, afraid that someone would overhear their discussion.

"I'm not a Heretic, not really, as you are so fond of reminding me," Douglas said as they walked toward their gate. "And this is a very different world we live in. I am surrounded by that evil every day. We see it on the street. I see it on a highly sophisticated level in Washington D.C. And I've been approached by those who want it stopped in our own government. And force can't be stopped with nice words. Force is stopped with force!"

Douglas had stopped in the middle of the walkway, just a little distance from their gate. He turned and faced Harris now, their faces just inches apart.

Harris looked calmly up at Douglas. He slowly shook his head.

"Douglas, you act as if you're the only one around here to see evil. I've seen enough evil in my life to sink an aircraft carrier. And I don't buy into the idea that you should meet force with force. You forget that we aren't fighting flesh and blood here. We're fighting Satan and his minions. And you don't fight demons with pistols and bullets."

"Regardless, there *will* be bullets flying," Douglas said. "And I don't want my wife or anyone I care about going in without protection. That's insanity."

"No," Harris said. "Insanity is believing you can do more than God can do. We are here to do His will. Let Him protect us."

"Ladies and Gentlemen, this is the international boarding call for American Airlines Flight 2122 to Salzburg, Austria...."

Harris looked at Douglas and raised an eyebrow.

"Let's continue this discussion later," Harris said.

"Absolutely," Douglas responded.

* * *

Salzburg, Austria

The meeting that Harris and Douglas had been invited to was scheduled for the Hyatt Regency in downtown Salzburg. Neither men had ever been to Austria, much less Salzburg, and they were tempted to do some sightseeing. But Harris was tired after their flight, and the presentation was scheduled for four hours later. The two of them checked in, with Harris taking a short nap while Douglas watched C-Span online.

An hour before the presentation, Douglas woke Harris, and he shaved, showered, and got dressed. Then they went downstairs to eat. They were met by Victor Vögel, the local representative who was organizing the event. It was a hastily conceived conference, only thought of a few weeks before, and so much of it was contrived at the spur of the moment. Even the meeting room where Harris was speaking was just now being set up with metal folding chairs and a small sound system. Vögel was profusely apologetic, and treated both Douglas and Harris like royalty, which Harris found embarrassing, and Douglas found amusing. Having been a U.S. Congressman, Douglas was more used to special treatment, but Harris wasn't.

The treatment continued, and actually increased as they entered the meeting room. Others had apparently read the book written by Michelle Kinkaid years before that had mentioned not only Harris and the ordeal he had gone through in prison, but many of the other Heretics as well, including Douglas. Some lined up for autographs, or to have their photos taken with Harris and Douglas, but Harris continued to push forward toward the stage.

The applause began even before Victor Vögel began speaking and continued over his words in English: "Ladies and gentlemen, Pastor Harris Borden!"

Harris Borden climbed the steps onto the platform amid loud applause from the small crowd. He looked out over the thirty-some people in the audience as he stood behind the microphone.

Douglas took a seat on a folding chair in the second row and stared at the man for a long while as he stood there, without doubt the most famous man in the room, yet still as unassuming as ever. The famous scar that identified him and marked his historic journey ran from beneath his left ear across his throat to the tip of his chin. At one time, Harris had worn a full beard to cover the scar, as if he were ashamed of it. But now, here in front of these men and women, Borden wore it like a badge of honor. It signaled a landmark in the journey that all of them had taken in the past twenty-five years.

"Our scripture today is one that you are all very familiar with," Borden said. "It's from Matthew 10:16: 'Behold, I send you forth as sheep in the midst of wolves. Be ye therefore wise as serpents and harmless as doves.'"

He paused for a moment to let the words sink in before continuing.

"We all know the setting behind these words. Jesus was about to send his disciples out into the world on their first missionary journey. He knew that they would not only have to deal with people who didn't like what they had to say, or who they were, or what they represented. That was bad enough. He knew that they would be dealing with Satan and his armies. Ephesians 6:12 spells it out: 'For our struggle is not against flesh and blood, but against the rulers, against the authorities, against the powers of this dark world and against the spiritual forces of evil in the heavenly realms.'"

* * *

Buenos Aires, Argentina

"¿Encontraste un piloto confiable?" Ernesto Gulliame peered into the hotel room where the two other teammates were gathering up their gear.

"English, Ernesto," Maria barked back at him. "Yes, we found a dependable pilot. Now for the last time, will you pick up the gear and get to the car? We're going to be late."

Ruiz shook his head. "I don't know why you insist on speaking English here in Argentina. We'll have plenty of opportunity to do it while we're in training."

"Best get in the habit of it," Maria sniffed. "As you say, you've had a lifetime to speak Spanish here at home. Now let's take advantage of this opportunity to learn American English."

"You betcha," Ernesto said, grinning. "Is that all, Princess?"

Ruiz laughed, and Maria turned red, then shook her head.

"Just get the bags," she said.

* * *

Tokyo, Japan

The shuttle bus to the airport was caught in the usual Tokyo traffic. The four young Christians sat in the back seat of the bus, looking at the scenery in the gathering darkness. The two young women talked and looked out the window. Ito Tamaguchi, the leader who had just celebrated his 25th birthday, looked at his watch again. They were going to be late. The older man, their chaperone, sat on the other side of him, reading his Bible. It was opened to Isaiah.

"God," Ito prayed quietly. "I put myself and these others in your hands."

* * *

Alexandria, Egypt

Solomon stood with the hood of the car opened, looking in mystery at a vehicle that wouldn't go. He wiggled a few wires and then shouted to Ibrahim, the young man behind the wheel.

"All right, try it now," he said. He heard the engine click.

"I don't understand," Solomon said. He looked back at the two others, who sat patiently in the vehicle, waiting for him. "It worked this morning."

"I am praying, my brother," Gamal said from the back seat.

Solomon smiled thinly. "I appreciate that greatly, Gamal. Perhaps God will send us a mechanic." He turned and looked down the busy street to see if one was coming.

* * *

Douglas watched the collection of church leaders from around the globe who had congregated to hear Harris this evening. When all this began, no one could have guessed where Harris' adventure would have taken them all, and no one could have imagined what was being proposed here. The concept was still so far-fetched that it was being kept under wraps away from most traditional church leaders. Only those who were innovative thinkers had been invited.

"So, let's get back to our original scripture, shall we?" Harris was saying up front. "'Be ye therefore wise as serpents and harmless as doves.' Most theologians interpret this phrase judiciously. 'Wise as serpents.' Are snakes really wise? We generally say this means we shouldn't take any risks. With our Christian brethren in many political situations, it usually means don't take sides. Don't rock the boat. Don't make waves. That way we can spend our efforts on spreading the gospel.

"Don't make waves," he said quietly, staring out at the audience, as if lost in thought. "Don't make waves."

"The trouble with that idea is that we live in a horrible, sin-filled, corrupt world," Harris said, his voice rising. "People suffer because we don't make waves. People die because we're afraid to rock the boat. I agree that most Christians shouldn't go looking for trouble. But I also believe that there is plenty of trouble that's out there, ready to look for them.

"That's where we come in."

* * *

Tokyo, Japan

Ito heard the roar of half a dozen high-powered motorcycles, sneaking between lanes on the freeway. Their roar grew louder as they drew up behind the shuttle bus. He heard a couple roar past, then he heard what sounded like a bump.

"What was that?" Yuki, who sat next to the window said.

"What was what?" Ito responded.

"It sounded like he put something on the side of the bus."

Ito stood up and looked, as the bikers roared away.

* * *

Buenos Aires, Argentina

Ruiz pulled through the gate to the private airport in the minivan and drove across the tarmac to the small hangar where their chartered jet stood. As they drove up, Maria jumped out of the passenger seat and Ernesto ran around to the back to get the bags.

"What's the pilot's name?" Ruiz asked, slamming the door, and heading for the hanger office.

"Lorenzo Pablon," Maria shouted after him. "Make sure his international pilot's license is up to date." Ruiz waved over his shoulder at her as she went to help Ernesto.

* * *

Alexandria, Egypt

"Look, look. Our prayers have been answered!" Gamal said. A small red Mitsubishi pickup pulled up in front of their car and two men in coveralls got out.

29

"Trouble?" the first man said.

"I don't understand it," Solomon said, standing in front of the raised hood. "It was running this morning."

"The Devil doesn't want us to get to the airport," Gamal shouted from the back seat.

"Maybe so," the first man said, pulling an automatic pistol out and pointing it at Solomon.

* * *

"More than twenty-five years ago, I asked God to be used in a bigger way," Harris was saying up front. "He responded by showing the evil that pervades this world. There are not only bad people in this world. Satan lives in this world. Demons rule this world. And the more we push, the more they will push back.

"Satan doesn't want good to succeed. He wants us to stay in our comfort zones, our protected little areas where we won't be harmed and yet we won't do any damage to his plans either. As long as we do nothing, he won't hurt us. It's when we try to do good, to shake up his plans, that Satan takes off the gloves.

"After I took on God's challenge, I started others on my path. I named them the Heretics because we chose a different path. Some think we're crazy for choosing the dangerous road. But there are many people who need our help. And we aim to help them.

"A few years ago, I was given the chance to step aside and lead a normal life. I went back to the wife and son I had left many years before. But after all that I had seen, it was impossible for me to put it all down. And so, I have been called for something bigger. *This.*"

Harris looked out at the small gathering of Christians from around the world.

"You've been asked to come here because all of you know a little of my story and have an inkling of what we all face. It's our plan to turn the Heretics into an international organization—with your help— and face evil wherever it raises its ugly head. As I speak, three teams from South America, Asia and Africa are on their way to training and then their assignments in their parent countries."

Douglas' eyes squinted as he watched Borden unfold the plan.

* * *

Buenos Aires, Argentina

"Ernesto?" Maria shouted into the empty hangar. She got no response. "Ruiz? Where are you guys?" Then she fell back into Spanish.

"*Dejen de jugar, amigos,*" she shouted. When she got no response, she felt a chill go up her back. She headed over to the office and opened the door.

Inside, the woman at the desk was sitting slumped over her computer, blood running across the keyboard. Maria gasped and turned to leave.

She never saw the man who killed her.

* * *

Alexandria, Egypt

Solomon backed away from the engine well slowly and joined the other two young men beside the car. When they saw the two dark men who held pistols on them, they had different reactions.

Gamal began to pray aloud, and Ibrahim scowled at the two men.

"We are called by God," Ibrahim said to them. "We aren't afraid of you."

"We don't care," said the second man. The first man shot Solomon in the chest, and then Ibrahim. Then they stood looking at Gamal, who continued to pray.

"Your prayers aren't going to help you," the man in front said.

"I'm not praying for myself," Gamal said. "I'm praying for God to forgive you."

The second man shot Gamal in the head, and then laughed.

* * *

Tokyo, Japan

"Pull over!" Ito began to shout to the bus driver. "We have to get out of this bus!"

"I can't pull over," the driver shouted back. "We're in the center lane and both lanes on either side are blocked."

"Then let us get out right here!" Ito shouted.

"Here! Are you crazy?"

"Here! Now! I think someone put a bomb on the outside of the bus!"

With those words, the bus driver slammed on the brakes and the bus came to a screeching halt right in the middle of rush-hour traffic.

"Everyone out! Everyone out!" Ito shouted in unison with the bus driver.

The people on the bus filed off quickly with Ito and the driver looking at each other as they came off the bus. Just as Ito's feet touched the pavement, the bus exploded.

The entire back of the bus flew into the air.

* * *

"I've made reference to the Heretics in years past as being God's spiritual Special Forces," Harris continued, a small smile on his lips. "But that title is very misleading.

"For the forces of evil can depend on their own strength and the power of the dark one. But if we depend on our own strength, it only draws us away from dependence on God. Our strength comes in weakness. We must be prepared for the onslaught that is inevitable if we face evil in the world. We must also face the fact that some of us may not survive that confrontation."

As he spoke, cellphones began to beep around the room, and people began to check texts.

"Tertullian wrote that 'the blood of martyrs is the seed of the church.' Well, that goes double for what we are doing. God is on our side. We may die doing what we are doing, but God will win. And that's what counts."

Douglas checked his own cellphone, and he saw what he suspected the others were seeing. Dead in Buenos Aires. Murdered in Egypt. Explosion in Japan. His lips became a thin line as he looked around the room at the others.

If he knew anything about human nature, most of them didn't hear a word Harris Borden said after the texts started coming in. And if those killed were from their countries, they were going to be open to considering other alternatives.

For as much as Douglas respected Harris Borden, he felt that there might come a time when a loaded weapon was necessary. 𝒱

4

The Deep End

"Connie," she heard behind her in the hallway, as she was walking away from Calligraphy class. Connie turned and saw the young, dark professor in a Brooks Brothers suit who had taught her comparative religion class the semester before walking swiftly toward her.

"Prof. Valencia," Connie said. "I'm surprised to see you over here in the Doty Fine Arts building. Didn't take you for the crafty sort."

Jorge Valencia smiled back at her. "Well, I did get a minor in fine arts. You should see my paintings. Some say my work is a lot like Gauguin's."

Connie's eyebrows raised. "I'm impressed. Yeah, I'd like to see that."

"But that's not why I stopped you," Prof. Valencia said. "I've been thinking about your presentation and your papers last semester in our comparative religion class. Very impressive. We need that kind of thinking to stretch the imaginations of our students. Far too many of them are stuck in the ruts of atheism, nihilism, or even a phony eastern mysticism without really exploring the borders of what's possible."

Connie's cell phone went off, its shrill ring interrupting her thinking, and she shut it off without looking. She hesitated. "I'm flattered…I guess. So, what do you have in mind?"

"You still haven't declared a major, and you're a sophomore. I checked. Seems like you need to come up with one. I'd like you to consider becoming a philosophy major."

Connie frowned. "Uh, let me ask the question that my parents are going to ask, and that I'm sure you've heard a million times. What can I do with a philosophy major?"

Connie's phone's shrill ring interrupted again, and she looked down to see who it was. She shut it off.

"Do you need to get that?" Prof. Valencia asked.

Connie shook her head. "It's just my sister. She's a linguistics professor in Dallas. She's probably wanting to bug me about some family thing."

"To answer your question, a philosophy degree is probably the most valuable undergraduate degree you can get these days. It teaches you to evaluate and think critically. You learn to evaluate arguments and claims of truth. Most of the students who study philosophy go on to have careers in teaching, banking, law or the ministry."

He paused and Connie stood in the hallway, thinking about it.

"In addition, you need to understand that it's my personal belief a college education is more important than just your degree. It helps you become the adult you were meant to be and contribute to society in a more meaningful way."

Connie nodded. "Can I think about it?"

"Well, Connie, if you decide to accept, I want you to consider two other things. First, you need to add a class this semester. Our entry-level philosophy class is required for all incoming majors. In addition, we have a conference scheduled for the end of the semester. I'd like you to consider being a part of it. It's called 'Science, Magic, or Faith.'"

"Sounds cool. What do you mean, 'be a part of it'?"

Prof. Valencia chuckled. "Okay, I'd like you to be one of the presenters. The presenters need to all be students from our department, and we need someone who is a believer to represent that perspective. Will you do it?"

Connie's phone went off again, and she threw up her hands in exasperation.

Prof. Valencia laughed and nodded. "I'll give you time to think about it." He waved and turned to go.

Connie switched her phone on.

"Yes, Maddie, what is it?" she asked, the irritation obvious in her voice.

"It took you long enough to answer the phone," Connie heard the voice of Dr. Madelyn Simms, linguistics professor at Chisholm Tech University. "Were you in the bathroom or something?"

"No, I do have a life," Connie barked. "If you must know, I was talking to a cute professor who was trying to persuade me to be a philosophy major."

"Well, that's all well and good, but I need you to get to the airport," Maddie said. "I have a ticket waiting for you at the Southwest Airlines front desk."

"What are you talking about?"

"Hurry, your flight is in two hours," Maddie continued. "You don't want to miss it."

"Why would I want to go to the airport?"

"Connie! You're not listening!" Maddie said. "Daddy's had a heart attack. You need to get home. I'll meet you when you get here."

Connie's mouth went dry, and she didn't answer for a second. Finally, she said, "Wait, what are you talking about?"

But her sister had already hung up the phone.

* * *

Gottfried Zimmer (Room)
Hyatt Regency Hotel
Salzburg, Austria

It took less than a minute for the entire room of thirty people to break into pandemonium. Harris Borden held his hands up and tried to calm the crowd, but he quickly realized that he had lost control. He stepped down from the small platform and met Victor Vögel, the program chair, and Douglas at the bottom. Douglas grabbed both men and pulled them to the side, while others quickly grabbed their belongings and headed for the exits.

"*Unmöglich!*" Victor Vögel hissed as they came together. "How could this happen? Three teams on three different continents. Wiped

36

out at the same time. Who could have such power? Who could have this kind of information?"

Douglas shook his head. "It can't be anyone on our end. No one with the Heretics knew where the teams were, including Harris and me." He looked at Harris, then back at Victor. "That brings it back to you and your people."

Harris shook his head. "It doesn't matter. The Devil has forces everywhere. He saw what we were planning on doing and realized that he needed to step in, quickly, and stop it. What matters most is what we do now."

Douglas looked at the quickly emptying room. "Well, whatever we do, it looks like we're alone again."

Victor looked around him, chagrined. "This is embarrassing. I thought we were better than this. I thought we were ready for this."

Harris smiled thinly. "No one is truly ready for it when it comes. We are very, very careful about the people we let into our inner circle. Now you see why."

Douglas pursed his lips. "So, what's the plan?"

Harris frowned and thought for a moment. "Alamo River."

Victor looked at Harris, confused, but Douglas nodded.

"I still have some government connections," Douglas said. "I'll touch bases with them and make my way home. It'll be safer."

Harris nodded. "I will head another direction. See you in a few."

Victor looked at the two men, up until a few minutes ago honored guests. Now they were pariahs, people that were dangerous to be around.

"What about me?" Victor said. "What should I do?"

Douglas looked at Harris, who turned to Victor.

"I suggest you take a vacation, starting today," Harris said. "Somewhere you've never been before. Stay there as long as you can afford to. And do a lot of praying.

"We'll all need your prayers."

As Douglas and Victor disappeared, Harris took the time to do one more thing. He sent a text on What'sApp to the group Heretics number. It read:

Six Alamo River 217-3347-2283.

* * *

Ramstein AFB, Germany
Four Hours Later

The Mercedes-Benz pulled up to the front gate of Ramstein Air Force Base, and the suited man in the front seat handed the uniformed soldier at the gate his identification.

"It's okay," the man said over his shoulder. Douglas sat up from where he had been lying on his seat and the soldier immediately put his hand on his sidearm.

"At ease, Airman," Douglas said. He handed the soldier his passport and his government ID. The soldier looked at the papers from the two people in the car, nodded and handed them back to the driver.

"You okay?" the driver asked Douglas as he brushed himself off after lying under blankets for four hours. "Need to freshen up?"

"Nah, I'm fine," Douglas said. "I bet you boys in the CIA do this often."

"Occasionally," the driver said. "A lot more fun that sitting behind a desk."

"I'm sure it is," Douglas said.

"My orders are to drive you straight over to the airstrip. Your Gulfstream leaves in fifteen minutes."

"Nice," Douglas said. "Thanks."

"My pleasure, Sir."

* * *

The Austrian-Czech Republic Border
That Same Time

Harris Borden traveled light, and he didn't believe in credit cards. That probably went all the way back to his first experience with the Universal Finance Corporation more than twenty years ago, the credit card company that ended up being a front for demonic activity. But in a practical manner, he also realized that people in his field of work needed as small a digital footprint as possible.

When he left the conference room, he didn't even bother to go back to his room to gather his things. Still wearing his suit, he stopped in the lobby of the hotel and used his debit card to withdraw the maximum amount of cash possible in euros. Then he made a quick but not-so-obvious getaway to the train station in Salzburg, where he caught the first train headed out.

In Weis, he switched over to the local train headed to Linz. In Linz, he switched again, this one headed for Prague, in the Czech Republic. It was his plan to switch trains several more times once he got into other countries. It cost more money, and he was at risk of being exposed by the many cameras that train stations used. But by stopping in small cities, he thought it was less likely someone would see him. In the meantime, he was trying to shake anyone following him.

To help with that, he talked a tourist—luckily from Ukraine, so he spoke Russian—into trading his slacks and casual shirt, along with his hat and glasses, for Harris' new suit. They switched in the tourist's private booth on the train, and they ended up having dinner together.

Now it was late, and Harris was alone on the train headed across the border into the Czech Republic. Despite everything he had been through over the years, Harris was stressed, more that other people were at risk than the fact that he was in danger. And like every other time that Harris was overwhelmed, he turned to his Bible for comfort.

But the words didn't seem to make sense to him. His thoughts were jumbled in his head, forming a barrier to the Holy Spirit's ability to comfort him. He shut his Bible and closed his eyes, praying.

"Lord, this is unlike anything we have ever faced," Harris said. "It's not enough for me to put myself in your hands and say, 'Your will be done.' Now we're talking about the lives of a dozen people that I care about very much. And we don't even know what it is we're facing, who they are, what they are, or what they want. Please," he said, tears coming to his eyes. "Please, help us."

He continued to pray, and slowly he began to feel better. He opened his Bible again and realized that the upper light in the cabin he was in had gone dark. He peered through the darkness and found the switch for the reading light above his seat. He pressed the button and immediately it shone on the open page of his Bible and spotlighted Matthew 5:13: "You are the salt of the earth. But if the salt loses its saltiness, how can it be made salty again? It is no longer good for anything, except to be thrown out and trampled underfoot."

Harris thought about the passage for a long time, and suddenly it all made sense. 𝒱

5

Alamo River

Six Alamo River 217-3347-2283.

Ruth and Josh knew what it meant, but the others were puzzled by the cryptic text message. Sitting in Ruth's living room, Taupe stared at Josh, then at Ruth quizzically.

"Come on, Ruth," Taupe said. "Tell us what it means."

"You should know what it means, Taupe," Josh said. "You were the one who first sent out the 'Helter Skelter' message."

"Yeah, I know," Taupe said. "'Helter Skelter' was pretty universal as a bug-out message. We all know that. But 'Alamo River'?"

"Well, think about it," Ruth said. "'Alamo' means coming together to hunker down and wait for instructions. Seems appropriate here in Texas, doesn't it?"

"Yeah, but 'Alamo River'?" Taupe asked. "There is no Alamo River."

"I've got it," Bobby finally said. He was on the intercom from downstairs, where he was staying with Ruth for the time being. "The last few numbers are IDs for online conference calling. River must mean streaming. As in video streaming."

"So, we have the message to gather online, probably Zoom, and he gave us an ID to find him," Ruth said aloud. "But when? Six something. Six hours? Or six days?"

"If it is urgent, then likely six hours," Bobby said. "By the way, guys, I'm getting some international news that doesn't look good."

"What?" Ruth said. "Tell us."

"A bus got blown up in rush hour traffic in Tokyo," Bobby said. "In addition, there was a mass murder at a small airport outside Buenos Aires. Looks like assassins."

Ruth bit her lip and looked at Josh.

"If he means six hours, we don't have long to wait," Ruth said. "Make sure the others know."

Ruth logged onto Zoom at the appropriate time, with Bobby logging on downstairs, and Josh and Taupe stood behind Ruth. Peewee was logged on elsewhere, as was Rojo. The faces of the Heretics made up a checkerboard on the screen, and in a happier time, they probably would have heard some joking about the Brady Bunch, or Hollywood Squares. But the faces were sober. As they watched, a black screen popped on, with Douglas' name on it, and finally another screen with Harris' image. It was dark where Harris was. It was obvious that he was broadcasting from his smartphone.

"Hi gang," Harris said. "Glad to see all of you here." He hesitated. "Where are the students?"

Ruth shook her head. "We tried contacting both of them. Connie disappeared suddenly, and Adam isn't carrying a phone because of his father." Adam Target's father was Ian Target, the billionaire who had caused trouble for the Heretics before.

Harris sighed. "Well, maybe it's best they're outside the circle. If they don't know what's going on, maybe they won't get hurt."

"Where are you, Harris?" Taupe asked from behind Ruth. "It's dark, but I see a lot of motion behind you."

"I'm on a train in eastern Europe," Harris said. "That's probably all I should tell you. The less any of you know, the better."

"What happened in Salzburg?" Josh asked.

"It's not what happened in Salzburg, it's what happened while we were in Salzburg." The words came from Douglas' blacked out screen. "Sorry my screen is blacked out. I'm headed back to the U.S., but I am on a state department plane, and they're pretty strict about what I can show."

"What does Douglas mean, Harris?"

42

Harris shrugged. "Someone told our competition about the teams. Someone powerful wants us dead. It's nothing new. But what's new is that we don't know who they are."

"Sure, we do," Josh said. "This smacks of Ian Target."

"Maybe," Harris said. "But this is a lot more sophisticated and organized than anything we've ever dealt with. Not only did they know where all three teams were, but when they were leaving. Douglas and I didn't even know that. And they were able to make their hits and get away without a trace."

"No," Bobby said. "There's no such thing as 'without a trace.' There's always a digital trail. I'll find them."

"That's my intention, Bobby," Harris said. "But we need to keep everyone safe in the meantime. They know where we are, but we don't know who or where they are." He paused and looked at the group.

"You're all veterans," Harris said. "You're used to working as teams. But I have new orders for you."

"Anything," Taupe said. "Just name it."

Harris looked down to the Bible in his lap. "Matthew 5:13 says: "'You are the salt of the earth. But if the salt loses its saltiness, how can it be made salty again? It is no longer good for anything, except to be thrown out and trampled underfoot.'"

"I read this a few hours ago, and it was as if God was telling me that we were like salt, congregated in one place for too long. It's time to spread out. It's time to work alone, to depend on the Holy Spirit more."

He looked at the group.

"I started out alone, just me and God. And it was a very lonely time. But it was also a time where I learned a lot, especially to depend on God instead of what I could do. So, here's what we're going to do.

"We are going to scatter. Each of you has a safety deposit box that was assigned to you long ago. In it is an envelope with some starting cash and directions as to where you are to go. There will be limited communication between you. Only I will know where you are. And I will be constantly on the move somewhere in Europe."

43

Harris took a few minutes for his words to sink in, waiting for questions from the group. Finally, Bobby spoke.

"What about me?" Bobby asked.

"Bobby, you have your command vehicle. I'm going to ask Peewee to go with you. Stay on the road as much as you can. I'll stay in close communication with you. Your priority is to find out whatever you can about this new force that is threatening us. Who it is, where it is, and where they will attack next."

Bobby nodded. "Got it, Boss."

"Is this going to be permanent?" Taupe asked, her voice strangely meek.

Ruth shook her head and looked over at her.

"Nothing's permanent, not even this world."

"No, I hope it won't be permanent," Harris said. "But I think we can do good in a lot of new places this way. And it will have fresh markings on it, your markings, with each of you new leaders wherever you go."

Taupe shook her head slowly. "I don't want to be a leader."

Josh chuckled. "Too bad, sister. You've been chosen."

Ruth looked down at her phone and saw a text from Douglas: *Pack your bags. I will call you in a few.*

She looked up at the screen and raised her hand.

"Harris, is there an assignment for me?"

He nodded. "You're still one of the Heretics, aren't you? If you have a deposit box, you get an envelope."

After they ended the Zoom call, Josh and Taupe headed for the bank, with the understanding that they wouldn't enter the building at the same time. She hugged the two of them for the last time, not sure when she would see them again. She lingered for a long time in her hug with Josh, her little brother.

"Be careful," she said quietly.

"Go with God," Josh replied. "I love you, Sis."

Peewee showed up with the RV a little after that, and Ruth said goodbye to him and Bobby.

"I won't ask where you're going," Ruth said, bending down to give Bobby a hug in his wheelchair.

"It wouldn't matter if you did," Bobby said. "I don't know myself. It's probably better that way."

She stood in the gravel driveway of her large home overlooking Lake Travis and wondered how long she would be there. Then she sighed to herself. No, nothing was permanent.

"Time to pack," she muttered, then sighed, turning back toward the door of the house.

As she was walking back to the house, her cell phone chirped, and she looked at it. It was Douglas.

"Hi, Sweetheart," she said, still walking toward the house. "What time do you expect to arrive in Austin?"

"I'm not flying to Austin," Douglas said. "I'm going straight to Washington. I've been in contact with our friend Sparky. You remember that job he talked to us about a while back?"

Ruth thought about what had happened in the past few months. How Senator Albert Bemis of New York had publicly harassed Douglas in his efforts to be approved by the Senate as the next Attorney General of the United States, yet had approached them secretly asking for their help. In years past, as a congressman, Douglas had chaired a presidential taskforce directed at rooting out corruption in the federal government. That taskforce had been disbanded when the new president had been elected. Now an online avatar by the name of "Sparky" was asking Douglas to work behind the scenes to reinstate the taskforce but do it quietly.

"Yeah, I remember," Ruth said. "Does this job offer come with housing and a 401K package?"

Douglas laughed. It was the first laugh that Ruth had heard since they had received the news of the attacks. It was refreshing.

"We'll work something out," Douglas said.

"Douglas," Ruth said. "Harris said he had an envelope for me too. What if he wants me to...to...."

"What if he expects you to go somewhere else?" Douglas completed her sentence. "Well, I guess you have to ask yourself. Are you a Heretic, or are you Mrs. Douglas Washington?"

Ruth's ears buzzed. She stopped walking and stared straight ahead.

"I can't believe you just said that," she said. "After all this time, all the group has been through. You are asking me to choose?"

"You really haven't been a Heretic for years now," Douglas said. "What are you? Their banker. You can do that from anywhere. And it's time we build a life out from under the shadow of Harris Borden. Seriously, you don't have to be a Heretic to do good in this world."

"Of course not, Douglas," Ruth said, still struggling to find words. "But are you seriously talking about turning our backs on Harris if he calls for us?"

"Let's not decide anything right now," Douglas said. "Austin has become a target, and I think Washington is going to be safer for us. Pack up your things—just the essentials—and head for the airport. I'll have someone come and get the rest of our things later. I've booked you on a flight in four hours. Your ticket is waiting for you."

She opened her mouth to respond, still not sure they were doing the right thing. But Douglas had already hung up on the other end.

Ruth stared at her phone and for the first time in years, swore as she realized the choice that was in front of her.

Ruth made one stop on her way to the airport. She had her Lyft driver wait at the curb while she ran, carrying a small package, into Garrison Hall, where Douglas had his small office as an adjunct professor in the history department. As small as his office was, there was an even smaller desk situated by the entrance that was reserved for Connie, who worked as his reader.

"Hi Jacob," Ruth said to Jacob Wilhite, the overweight senior who worked as the assistant at the front desk as she breezed by. "I just need to drop something off in my husband's office."

"Prof. Washington said he would be gone for an extended period," Jacob told her. "He'll be finishing his classes online."

Ruth nodded. "Yes, I know. I have something for his reader."

Jacob kept talking as Ruth walked quickly down the hallway to his office. The door was locked.

"Jacob, would you be a sweetie and unlock the office door for me?" she shouted back down the hallway. Jacob came hustling toward her a moment later, rattling a ring of keys.

"I haven't seen Constance for a day or two," Jacob said. "Is she traveling with Prof. Washington?"

"No, she's not," Ruth said, as he opened the door. She reached under her arm and pulled out the small bag with clothing in it and placed it on Connie's desk. Then she reached into her purse and pulled out a card and laid it on top of the package.

"Make sure this room stays locked until either Connie or Prof. Washington comes back. Okay, Jacob?" Ruth said to him. Jacob nodded.

"That package is safe in here," Jacob said, smiling.

Ruth patted him on the shoulder. "Thank you, Jacob. Be good." She left the office and headed back to the waiting Lyft ride and the airport, realizing she likely would never see Jacob again.

* * *

Dallas-Love Field
Dallas, Texas

The Southwest Airlines flight from Austin was on time, and as usual, Connie packed light. She breezed right through baggage check with her carry on and headed straight out to the curbside, where her sister waited. Dr. Madelyn "Maddie" Simms, professor of ancient civilizations and ancient languages at Chisholm Tech University, was twelve years older than Connie, and a beautiful, confident, sometimes overbearing world-famous researcher and lecturer.

Maddie beeped the horn of her double-parked Honda Civic and Connie ran between cars to join her. The foggy day had turned into a misty rain. Connie opened the back passenger door and threw her small suitcase in the back seat, then jumped in the front seat next to her sister. Connie started to learn forward to hug her, but Maddie instead looked in the rearview mirror from the driver's seat and immediately pulled out into traffic.

"So," Maddie said, her face blank.

"So," Connie said, a slight smile coming onto her face. *"In che tipo di guai ti sei cacciato ultimamente?"*

"Italian, huh?" Maddie said, joining her in a grin. "We're playing that game, are we? *Iaqad kunt 'aetani bieamlik."*

"No fair," Connie said. "You know I don't speak Arabic. At least not yet. Try this one: *Goodshtë mirë të jesh në shtëpi."*

Connie grinned, and Maddie's eyes lit up. "That's a new one. Hmm, let's see. Serbian? No, Albanian."

"Good guess," Connie said. "My roommate's from Albania. I've known her all of three months. She's learning English and I'm learning a new language. With Mandarin that I'm currently studying, that'll make twelve." She looked at Maddie for a long moment. "I said, 'It's good to be home.'"

Maddie reached over and patted Connie's wet jeans leg as she drove.

"It's good to have you home. If it were up to me, you'd be here all the time."

Connie turned away and looked out the window at the drizzling rain that ran off her window. "How is Daddy doing?"

"Better," Maddie said. "It was mostly a scare for all of us. Fortunately, I was in town, just finishing a lecture when Mama called me. He was cleaning out the roof gutters, for land's sake! He had just come into the house, and complained that he didn't feel right. He sat down in his chair in the living room and then it happened. It could have been a lot worse."

"What hospital is he in?"

"Providence," Maddie said. "Mom wants to stay there with him tonight, but I can tell she's tired. She and I have been taking turns sitting with him. They're monitoring him pretty closely." She glanced over at Connie. "I'm taking you straight to the hospital."

Connie nodded. "Understood."

Maddie sniffed and her mouth became a thin line. "You know, this whole thing would be a lot simpler if you had chosen to go to college here in Dallas instead of going to Austin. I really don't know what you're trying to prove."

Connie looked out her window again. "Do we really need to have this conversation again?"

"I wanted to have it when it was just the two of us," Maddie said. Connie looked at her, and Maddie could see the pain in her sister's eyes. "I know you think you have to get out from under my shadow. But your family needs you too. I can't be here all the time. I have a career. I have a lot of people who depend on me, and I travel a lot. If you were here...."

"If I was here, you wouldn't have to worry about the 'rents, right?" Connie said. "You could turn everything over to little sister, is that it?" Connie tried hard to keep her voice level, but the stress of hearing of her father's heart attack was coming out in her wavering voice.

"Well, believe it or not, I have a life too," Connie continued. "I have people who depend on me too. There's a group of Christians who are doing good things in Austin—everywhere, really—and they have asked me to train to be one of them. It's a big responsibility, and it's more than just family, but it's what I want to do."

"Who are these people?" Maddie said. "Why haven't you talked about them before?"

"Well, they're sort of secret," Connie said. She hesitated, as if trying to decide how much to tell her sister. "They're called the Heretics."

Maddie scoffed. "The what? Ridiculous. Sounds like a cult. How can they be more important than taking care of your family?"

"Don't you understand? *They're* my family now!" Connie's voice grew louder.

"Then why in blazes did you come home?" Maddie screamed back at her sister. "Don't you understand? Your father could die! Don't you want to do something about it?"

Connie shook her head, tears coming. "Of course I do. I wouldn't be here if I didn't. But you're much closer. You have your life and I have mine. Why can't you just accept that?"

Maddie sighed heavily. "You're still just a kid. You don't know. How will you feel if you lose him?"

"Oh, that's just great," Connie said, folding her arms over her chest and sinking down in her seat. "Guilt always works."

They were silent for a long while as they traveled through the Dallas traffic, Connie staring at the cars and buildings, blurred through the increasing rain and the tears that she struggled to keep from coming. Finally, Maddie spoke again.

"You say you're in training with these Heretics," she said. "How is that going?"

"Fine," Connie said quietly. "Actually, terrible. I'm doing great on all the brain stuff, the thinking stuff, but when it comes to the physical training, I'm a klutz. I have two left feet."

Maddie didn't respond for a long moment, then said.

"Well, maybe that's a message from God that you've chosen the wrong path. Just think about it, would you?"

I have been thinking about it. More than you can imagine, Connie thought to herself. But she wasn't willing to share that with her sister. She remained quiet for the remaining few minutes until they got to Providence Hospital and their father. ❮

6

Crossroads

Dallas, Texas

It was late by the time Connie and Maddie got to Providence Hospital. Maddie led Connie straight up to the CICU. The glass doors to the CICU were locked, and Maddie gestured to a phone on the wall.

"Mama's probably in there already," Maddie said. "They only allow two visitors at a time, so I'll wait out here. You'll need to call and identify yourself, and they'll let you in."

Connie nodded, a little intimidated by the strange situation. Her father, Mathias, had always been so strong. He rarely was sick, and never believed in showing weakness. But lately she had noticed him growing thinner and grayer, as had Mama. *Should she be staying home?* she asked herself. *Was it wrong for her to go off to Austin, to have her own life, to feel that God was calling her to do something completely different?*

She thought of this as she got on the phone and called the CICU nurses' station and waited for them to buzz her in. When the big glass doors whooshed open, she went through and immediately saw a sign: "All visitors must wash hands." She stopped at a sink and washed her hands with soap before proceeding. The nurse on the phone had told her that Mathias was in Unit 3, so she wandered down the eerily lit hall filled with the sounds of beeping equipment until she saw her mother sitting at the side of a bed. There, surrounded by equipment, wires, and tubes, was her father, his eyes closed, his face gray.

Alina Simesçu turned as Connie came in, and they hugged. Connie's tears began to fall, and Alina muttered quietly to her in Romanian.

"*O să fiu bine,*" her mother said. "*Va fi bine.*"

Connie's tears became a waterfall as she fell into her mother's lap, and she began sobbing uncontrollably. The two women held each other for a long time, not saying anything, just allowing mother and daughter to love each other without words. Finally, the sobbing subsided, and Alina Simesçu, the resourceful woman that she was, pulled a small packet of tissues from her coat pocket and handed them to Connie.

Connie sniffed and laughed, then nodded her thanks. She wiped her eyes and blew her nose. "I didn't mean for this to happen," she said, her tissue on her face muffling the words. "I was going to be the strong one. All of you always see me as the baby of the family, the one who needs to be taken care of. I wanted to show you that I was all grown up. And then…this happens." She looked at her mother through red eyes, then looked at her sleeping father.

"How is he doing? What do the doctors say?"

"They say that it was fortunate he was in the living room when it happened," Alina said. "Five minutes before, he was on the roof. *Doamne!* I can't imagine if this had happened when he was up there!"

"Will he need to have surgery? When can he go home?"

Alina shook her head. "Tests, tests, and more tests. They know it is his heart, but they do not know how bad it is. Maybe tomorrow we will know more."

Connie looked at her mother, a woman she always considered so strong. She and Mathias had escaped from Communist Romania with a small daughter and built a life in America with literally nothing but the clothes on their backs. Now they had one grown daughter with an international reputation and two PhDs, and another who was in college studying…what? Going…where? Connie stared at her mother and saw that her mother had grown smaller over the years, and tonight she seemed gray and frail, older than ever.

"Mama, why don't you let me stay here tonight and watch over Daddy?" Connie said. "You look like you could use some sleep."

"Oh, no," Alina said. "I couldn't leave him. I need to be here."

"Nonsense," Connie said. "You need rest. Tomorrow is a big day. Lots of tests, and probably lots of decisions to make. Maddie is in the waiting room. Go join her and go home. I'll be fine."

Alina hesitated, then put her hand up to touch Connie face, nodding reluctantly.

"You are growing up," Alina said, smiling slightly. "I see that. God is using you."

Connie smiled back at her mother, then kissed her cheek. "Go home, get some rest."

Alina stood up wearily and pulled her coat and purse from the back of the chair. She hesitated before leaving.

"I will be back first thing tomorrow," Alina said, then she was gone.

"Good," Connie said quietly, turning to her sleeping father. "That gives us a chance to talk. Just you and me, Daddy."

She sat down in the chair where her mother had been seated and scooted it up close to the bed where her father lay. She watched him breathe for a long while, his chest rising and falling, in sync with the reassuring beeps that came from the monitor on the other side of the bed.

"Daddy, you've always been the one who understood," she started quietly. "I need that right now. I need someone I can talk to. I feel called by God to do something, but it seems like the whole world is telling me I'm not the right person to do it. That I'm unqualified. That I'm just a kid. That I should be at home or studying like a good student.

"But someone—I really think it's the Holy Spirit—is telling me something else. I really feel like it is calling me to help people. Not tomorrow. Today. Sure, I know that I can help people here at home, with donations and by being kind to my neighbors. I know that you and Mama need help at home. But this is something different."

She paused and looked at her sleeping father while she gathered her thoughts.

"It's like what Abraham went through. God told him to leave his home and go on the road, taking only his wife, Sarah. He didn't even tell them where they were going. That's the way I feel. I feel like there's a big world out there that God wants me to meet, to help, to talk to about Him. And I'm scared, Daddy."

She began to cry and leaned over against her father.

"I know what you would say," Connie continued. "You would tell me that it's okay to be afraid, as long as you agree to trust God. And I do trust Him. He's already shown me that He is trustworthy. I just need the courage to do what needs to be done. More than anything, I need to know…." She hesitated and bit her lip. "I need to know that I'm not letting you and Mama down."

Connie turned and looked at the form of her sleeping father, who lay with wires and tubes running from him, his face grayer than she had ever seen it. As she looked at it, tears started to form in her eyes again, but she rubbed her face and fought them back.

"Stop it," she said to herself. "No time for pity. Others need you. You have to be strong."

As if in response, there was a rap on the wall beside the large glass opening that served as a doorway. A muscular young man in his mid-20s stood there in blue scrubs.

"Hi, I'm Byron, your Dad's nurse for this shift. I'm wondering if there's something I can get for you. Maybe something to eat or drink?"

"Eat? Drink?" Connie echoed, her mind dull.

"Yeah, the patients here in CICU usually can't have food or drinks themselves, but family is often here long term. The staff here gets fed by the cafeteria, so one of the perks the hospital has is that we offer the dinner tray that they serve the other patients to our visitors. They are featuring Salisbury steak tonight. It's pretty good."

Connie wrinkled up her nose. "I'm a vegetarian."

Byron shrugged. "How about we get you a salad? And some veggies?"

Connie's stomach rumbled and she realized she hadn't eaten since breakfast. She nodded.

"Sounds good," she said. "Thanks."

Connie sat back in her chair and held her father's hand, just looking at him for a long while. A few minutes later, Byron returned with the dinner tray. Sure enough, in lieu of Salisbury steak, Byron had substituted extra green beans and carrots, and an extra-large salad.

While Connie ate her meal, Byron adjusted the equipment monitoring Mathias, changed his drip line, and checked the catheter.

"Your mom says you're a student in Austin," Byron said as he worked. "You at UT?"

Connie nodded, her mouth full of green beans. "Yup. Sophomore."

"What's your major?"

Connie shrugged. "Not sure."

Byron chuckled. "Seems like you should be deciding that pretty soon, shouldn't you?"

"Probably." Connie was uncomfortable with the conversation, so she decided to change the subject. "How do you think my Dad is doing?"

"He had a rough go of it when he came in here," Byron said. "But he's stable now. Tomorrow morning, they plan on doing some tests. Right now, the important thing is that he rests, so we have him medicated so he'll sleep." He paused as he was about to leave the room.

"I can bring you some blankets," he said. "And that chair pulls out into a pretty comfortable bed."

"Thanks," Connie said, and handed him her dinner tray.

It was Connie's plan to stay up all night, watching her father and making sure he was all right. But after about an hour, it became obvious that nothing was going to change, he was in great hands with the CICU staff, and that she was tired from the flight up. So she took advantage of the blankets and the fold-out chair that became a bed, and she went to sleep herself.

Not long after that she began to dream.

Connie walked along one of the many alleys she had seen in Austin, often where the homeless congregated, trying to stay warm and dry at night. It was night, and she was alone. She was wearing a denim jacket that she didn't recognize, with her hands stuffed in the pockets. It was very dark, and as she walked down the alley, it seemed to get darker and darker.

Suddenly there was a rattling noise behind her and she turned to see what it was. A beat-up metal garbage can fell over, its contents falling onto the ground. As she looked at it, she thought she saw a blur of motion in the corner of her eye, and she turned to see what it was. When she did, she heard a glass bottle fall and break behind her on the pavement. She turned and saw a black cat running down the alley. Then she heard a rumble. She turned and something big pushed her off her feet.

She was lying on the street, water and trash littered around her. She started to pick herself up off the pavement, when she saw someone standing on the railing of a fire escape high above her. He was a spindly young Black man, in his teens, with orange spiky hair dressed in a black hoodie and jeans. He was perched on the edge of the fire escape as if he were a bird.

"What are you doing there?" Connie asked him.

The man grinned back at her. "I'm waiting for you, Connie," he said. "Waiting for you to save me."

He then leaped straight out into the alley and the darkness.

"Wakey, wakey," Connie heard the next morning. She opened her eyes and saw that a glimmer of light was streaming through the venetian blinds on the window. Her sister Maddie was standing at the doorway, with her mother behind her.

"What time is it?" Connie said, stretching. She sat up and slipped on her shoes.

"Seven-thirty," Maddie said. "You might want to slip out and get some food at the cafeteria while they're still open. Did you get anything to eat last night?"

Connie nodded, still rubbing her face. "Byron, the night nurse, brought me a tray."

"Ooh, Byron, is it? Was he tall and handsome?" Maddie said.

"Maybe," Connie said, grinning. "But I'm not interested." She stood and stretched. "I do need to use the restroom."

"Here," Alina said, handing her a small bag. Connie looked inside and saw her toothbrush and some toothpaste. "I thought it might make you feel better."

"Thanks, Mama," Connie said. "I'm surprised they let both of you in here. I thought the rule was only two visitors at a time."

"Shh," Maddie said, grinning. "They must have forgotten about you. Anyway, I'm about to leave town, and I wanted to say bye before I left."

"Leave? Leave where?"

"I'm a speaker at a conference in Miami," Maddie said. "Don't worry, I'll be back in three days."

"What?" Connie said. "I don't believe you! You called me about what an emergency this was, rushed me up here to Daddy's bedside, only so you can leave?" She shook her head at her sister. "You're impossible."

Maddie smiled condescendingly. "Connie, this conference has been planned for six months. I'm the main speaker. I can't get out of it. Like I said, I'll be back in three days. Mama knew about it. She'll keep me informed."

Connie fumed. "That's why you were in such a hurry to get me up here. That's why you need me to live here in Dallas. It's so you don't have to worry about things!"

Alina held up her hands and hissed at the two young women.

"*Opre te-te chiar acuma!* Stop it! Your father is lying here in this hospital bed, and you are making fools out of yourselves! I am ashamed of you! *Să vă fie rușine!*"

Instantly the fighting stopped between the two of them, but Maddie glowered at Connie for a long moment. Connie finally broke the silence, muttering, "I have to go to the bathroom," and rushed out of the room.

Connie went down four floors to the main entrance of the hospital, looking for a restroom. Instead, she found herself walking out the front door of the hospital and walking down the street. The cold morning air hit her like a slap on the face, but it helped her wake up. Her mind was flooded with a mixture of feelings: guilt for leaving her father's bedside, anger for being taken advantage of by her sister, and the persistent calling of Something Else. She used the walk down the street to help sort out her thoughts, and she didn't even really look where she was going until she saw the familiar Starbucks sign in front of her. She decided to go in and get a coffee.

She ordered a black coffee and a cranberry muffin and sat down at a corner table to think. *Help me sort this out, God*, she prayed silently. *Was it this hard for Abraham?*

She was staring at nothing, letting her coffee cool when a tall, blonde-haired man in his 30s in a suit and an overcoat approached her.

"Mind if I share your table?" he asked politely.

Connie shrugged. "Sure. Don't mind me. I've got stuff to think about."

The man sat down. "Thinking about Abraham, I suspect."

Connie's forehead furrowed. "What?"

"You asked for help sorting things out, didn't you, Connie?"

Connie suddenly got nervous. "Who...who are you?"

"Harris Borden knew me as The Messenger," the man said. "You can call me whatever you want."

Connie's heart began beating loudly in her chest. She looked around her at the busy coffee shop to see if anyone else had heard what this strange man was saying. He chuckled.

"Don't worry," The Messenger said. "This is just between us. They don't even know we're having this conversation."

She stared at the tall, almost beautiful, man. *Or was he a man?*

"So are you...are you...an...*angel?*"

The Messenger grinned. "That's what people on earth call me, I guess. Like I said, I go by a lot of different names. I've been around a long time and been a lot of places." He looked around at the people, focused on their smartphones and laptops. "I think this is my first visit to Dallas, however."

"But why...why me?" Connie asked. "Harris was special. I'm not special."

The Messenger chuckled. "In His eyes, every person is special. It comes down to whether you are willing to be used by Him or not. That's really the deciding question."

Connie looked at The Messenger and realized they were at an important moment in her life.

"What do you mean, 'the deciding question'?" she repeated.

The Messenger got a faraway look in his eyes as if trying to remember a distant memory. Then his eyes lit up.

"Mary…Moses…Peter…Samuel…Samson. I can list a hundred more names," he said. "Names you are familiar with because you read about them, and other names you never heard simply because they were never written down. But all of them had the chance to do something significant, and all of them had the chance to say yes, or no. I could add your friend Harris Borden to that list. Heaven has its own list, you know. Some were remembered by men for their brave deeds. Some were never known beyond a few people who appreciated what they did. And of course, Heaven knew. There are no guarantees of human thanks or recognition for what you do. But that's not why these people did what they did, of course. And it all goes back to that first, simple decision.

"Do you want to be used by God? It made all the difference in the world for Harris Borden, and it will make all the difference for you."

Connie stared at him for another moment before nodding.

"Yes," she said. "Definitely. I want that more than anything."

"I have to warn you, just as I warned Harris, that the road is not easy. There will be times of extreme pain and trouble. You might get hurt. People you love might get hurt. But God will never leave you."

The Messenger stood up to go.

"Wait," Connie said, looking up at the tall man. "Is that it? Aren't you going to tell me what to do now?"

The Messenger smiled and tipped his head. "You already know what to do."

Connie sat there with her coffee and muffin and watched The Messenger walk away. 𝒱

7

Alone

Connie stared at The Messenger's form as he walked down the sidewalk and out of sight, waiting to see him disappear in a puff of smoke, or ascend into heaven in a cloud, or better yet, sprout a pair of wings and fly away.

Instead, he continued down the sidewalk until he rounded a street corner and disappeared. The whole experience made her wonder if he had really been an angel, and then a moment later, whether it had even happened or not. She frowned and looked around her at the people who were caught up in their personal lives, some with laptops open and others busy talking on their phones. She leaned over to the teen girl who was across from her drinking a cappuccino and listening on her earphones and tapped her on the shoulder.

"Excuse me," Connie said, "did you see the tall, blonde man who came and talked to me just now?"

The girl shook her head. "I didn't see anyone. I thought you were alone."

Connie frowned and looked at the other customers around her, wondering if anyone else had seen him. But everyone seemed to be engrossed in their own worlds. Finally, she threw her cup and napkin in the trash and walked up to the barista behind the counter.

"Did you see the man who was just talking to me?" she asked him.

The tall, skinny 20-something man shook his head. "We get a thousand customers a day in here. I can't remember every guy."

Connie nodded. "Thanks." She turned, confused, and decided to walk back to the hospital. *Well*, she thought. *I guess this is where faith comes in*. God had just spoken to her through His Messenger, telling her that He was willing to use her if she was willing to be used. Who was she to doubt now?

But what did that mean as far as her family was concerned? She still needed to decide what she was going to do about her parents. God wanted her to go back to Austin, she had no doubt of that, but what kind of daughter would she be to abandon her parents in their time of need?

She was still mulling over this issue when she got back to the coronary intensive care unit. She buzzed the nurses' station to see if Maddie was still there and was relieved when the nurse said that only her mother was with her father. They let her in, and she washed before joining her parents at Unit 3.

Connie was surprised to see her father sitting up in bed when she arrived. The color had returned to his face, and he seemed animated and looked like he felt a lot better. Mathias and Alina were chatting together in Romanian, holding each other's hand while they talked. Connie's mother Alina looked a lot more relieved, and she smiled when Connie came in.

"*Draga mea,*" Alina said, "we were just talking about you."

"Hello Daddy," Connie said, coming up close and grasping Mathias' free hand. "How are you feeling?"

"*Mult mai bine,*" he said. "Much better. In fact, the doctor came in while you were gone. They will still run some tests today, but he's optimistic that I'll be able to go home, perhaps as early as tomorrow."

"That's wonderful," Connie said. "But we don't want to rush it. We want to be careful about this."

Mathias nodded. "We will, of course. But I don't want you to worry. You have your own life to take care of."

Connie opened her mouth to protest, but Mathias held up one hand and she closed it.

"You know, it's amazing the things one can hear if you're just quiet once in a while," he said, a slight smile on his face. "Like when your youngest, prettiest daughter comes to see you and thinks you're asleep and pours her heart out to you." He reached out and put his hand, tubes attached to the top of it, up to her cheek.

61

"You heard that?" Connie said, somewhat shocked. Mathias smiled back and nodded.

"You are being called by God," he said, looking into her eyes. "My darling daughter, that is all we have wanted for both of you. When the Lord calls, we want you to be like Samuel and say 'Speak, for your servant is listening.'" He looked at Alina. "And your mother and I never want to be in the way of that calling."

"But you're sick! You need my help!" Connie said, tears coming to her eyes.

"Are you trying to tell yourself that your parents are more important than God?" Alina said. "*Să vă fie rușine!* Shame on you!" She looked at Mathias. "We will take care of each other, and we have faith that God will take care of us as long as He needs us here."

"And when our time on earth is done," Mathias added. "You will be sad to see us go, but we will be resting, peacefully, in Jesus."

Connie stared at her parents, tears flowing freely down her face.

"I love you two so much," she said quietly, and hugged them both.

Several hours later, she was back in Austin. She'd caught a flight from Love Field in Dallas and emailed Adam to pick her up at the airport. He caught her outside baggage claim in his BMW just as the sun was going down.

"Hey," he said to her, jumping out to grab her bag from her and throw it in the trunk.

"Hey, yourself," she said, suddenly and impulsively reaching out and hugging him. Surprised, he hugged her back. She laughed nervously.

"Don't get the wrong idea, bucko," Connie said. "I just needed a hug. You're still in the doghouse."

"Understood," he said. He slammed the trunk door shut and they climbed into the front seat of the car. He put it in gear, and they drove out into traffic.

"How is your dad doing?" Adam asked, looking in the rearview mirror.

"Better," Connie said. "It wasn't easy leaving, but they gave their blessing."

"Really," Adam said. "What did your sister say?"

"I could care less what my sister has to say," Connie muttered, looking out the window. She sighed loudly.

"Oh, so it's going to be like that, is it?" Adam said, raising an eyebrow.

"Yeah, well, you could say we didn't see eye to eye," Connie said, still looking out the window. "She rushed me up there, only because she didn't want to feel guilty about not being there herself."

"The way you describe her, she's got a pretty busy life," Adam said. "She's pretty important."

"And I'm not?" Connie said. "I'm busy too."

Adam chuckled. "Sure you are."

"Listen, let's not talk about it anymore," Connie said. "My life is here. God has called me here. With the Heretics."

Adam cleared his throat.

"What?" Connie asked. "Did something happen?"

"They're gone."

"Who? Who's gone?" Connie suddenly felt her heart catch in her throat.

"Everybody," Adam said quietly. "I came to the bookstore yesterday and Josh was gone. This morning he didn't show up, so I tried calling everyone. No one answers. Nobody."

Connie frowned. "Well, surely they left a note."

Adam shook his head. "If I would have had a phone, I probably would have gotten a message from them. What about you?"

Connie pulled out her phone and looked at the messages. There were two of them. One was from an unlisted international number. The other was from Ruth. She listened and they both had the same exact message: *"Six Alamo River 217-3347-2283."*

She put it on speaker phone and played it for Adam. They looked at each other in confusion as they played it again and again.

"What does it mean?" Connie asked Adam. Adam stared blankly back at her.

He drove as fast as he could back to Reborn Books west of the university campus. Adam unlocked the door and they entered, not bothering to switch the sign from Closed to Open.

"There's got to be some kind of sign here," Connie said. "Some indication of where he went."

"Nothing," Adam said. "All of his clothes are still here. His van is still parked out back. His desk and computer are untouched."

"Have you checked his computer?" Connie asked.

Adam shook his head. "Passworded. And before you ask, he's not the kind to use "1-2-3" or "Password" as his password. It will take me some time to hack it."

"If you can't, I know a student or two here who can," Connie said. She looked up and realized that she had offended Adam. "Sorry. I have the utmost confidence in your abilities."

They looked around for another fifteen minutes before Connie threw up her hands.

"This is useless," she said. "Let's try Taupe's dojo. Maybe she left something there."

But Taupe wasn't at her dojo on Guadalupe Street, where she taught aikido and tai kwon do to college students as well as yoga to the older public. Her bookkeeper and assistant had just opened the doors for the evening and was just as surprised as they were that Taupe wasn't there for her evening classes.

"I'm not sure when she'll be back," Connie told Emily, the assistant. "Can you lead out while she's gone? I am sure she will be back in a few days."

"Oh-kay," Emily said, "but this is very strange. After all, she could have left me a note. Or called. Or texted." Connie could tell that Emily was feeling taken advantage of.

"I'm sorry this happened, Emily," Connie said. "We're just as confused as you are. As soon as we get some information, we'll share it with you. I promise. In the meantime, it's up to you and us to hold the fort, okay?"

Emily nodded, and they left.

Adam looked at Connie. "Shall we check Prof. Washington's house next?"

Connie shook her head. "It's a long way over to Lake Travis, and I suspect that they've left that as well. Let's check his office and see if he left a note for me there."

Adam and Connie got back in his BMW and drove down Guadalupe to Garrison Hall. He let her out on the street corner, and Connie told him to just drive around the block, knowing that parking was impossible to find that late in the evening.

She passed the elevator and bounded up the stairs to the third floor, surprised to see Jacob Wilhite still sitting at the front desk of the history department office suite.

"Jacob!" Connie said. "Isn't it a little late for you to be here?"

"Oh, hi Constance," Jacob said, blushing. Connie had known for a while that Jacob had a crush on her. "Mrs. Washington—the professor's wife—left something for you in the professor's office. It's on your desk." He rose quickly from his desk, grabbing his large ring of keys and hastily trying to rush for the hallway.

"How is your father doing?" Jacob asked.

"How did you know about my father?" Connie asked. "I only told Adam."

"Well, when you didn't check in yesterday or today, I called him," Jacob said. "I was worried you had caught this new virus everyone is getting. You know it's pretty bad." He walked stiff legged down the hall toward the office.

"And Adam told you?"

"Well not at first," he said, as he fumbled with the keys at the door. "I called Prof. Washington first, but he didn't answer. Then I called your roommate, and she didn't know. And then I called the lady that teaches you yoga—you know, she scares me sometimes...." He continued to fumble with the keys. "No, that's not the right one."

"You know, Jacob, I have my own key."

"Please, let me do this, Constance," he said. Connie could see that he was red in the face and sweating and nervous, so she backed off. "I took this job because I wanted to help people. I take great joy in helping people, especially…especially people like you." His voice died out and he slowed down in his fumbling of the keys. Suddenly his fingers latched on one gold one.

"Here it is!" Connie watched sweat drip from his forehead as he stuck the gold key into the lock and turned it. The door to Prof. Douglas Washington's office swung open, and Jacob looked up in triumph.

Connie clapped her hands. "Good job, Jacob. Thank you." She pushed her way past him to the office. She immediately saw the package and the card in a blue envelope on her small desk. She switched on the light to read it better. She opened the card and read:

"Can't say much. Wear this. It could save your life. Much love. -R"

Connie put the envelope down and opened the package. Inside was a blue denim jacket that looked like something a woman would wear at a country-western bar. She noticed that it was deceptively heavy for a denim jacket. On the back of the jacket, sewn in silver sequins were the words: "Eat at Joe's."

Connie stared at the jacket for a long minute before she put it on and turned to Jacob.

"Thank you, Jacob," she said, and left the office.

* * *

33rd Floor, The Broadgate Tower
London, England

Ian Target was no stranger to London. He had been there many times, both for business and for pleasure. It was one of the perks of being a billionaire that you could travel pretty much anywhere in the world without thinking about the cost of it, often at a moment's notice, stay at the swankiest hotels and eat at the best restaurants. You got used to it. And Ian Target missed it. Because Ian Target, as he often had to remind himself, was now a wanted man. He was sought by both the FBI and Interpol for his involvement in kidnapping and assassination plots in Texas. Fortunate for Target, he had a security staff who worked to keep him two steps ahead of law enforcement.

So even though Ian could no longer stay in public hotels, he did travel. But it took a little more coordination. After the conference with the Consortium in Eilean Donan a few weeks before, he had stayed with McArthur Henson in Scotland. But now he was in London, admittedly a dangerous place for him, on a quest to get something that he needed from someone more powerful than he ever imagined a person could be.

The elevators opened at the penthouse on the 33rd floor of The Broadgate Tower, and two very large men in suits immediately reached for Target to frisk him. His own security team was waiting downstairs, a stipulation he had agreed to before taking the elevator ride to the top of the skyscraper.

"Ian!" he heard from the other side of the room. The two men on either side of him released him and Target stumbled forward. He stepped out of the small foyer by the elevator and saw the room open up with floor to ceiling windows overlooking the skyline. It was breathtaking, with a bright, sunny day adding to the spectacle.

"Come here, old bean," Veritas gestured from the other side of the room. "Let Pedro fix you a drink. What will you have?" He nodded at the bar on the right side of the room where a bartender stood waiting expectedly.

"Scotch on the rocks would be nice," Target said. Pedro nodded.

"Come, look at this," Veritas said, gesturing once again at the view from the window. "Look at the world we've inherited."

Ian Target joined him, and a moment later, Pedro brought him his drink. All of London lay scattered beneath their feet.

"Eight million people out there, right below us," Veritas said. "And they'll do whatever we ask them to. The most beautiful women will beg to make love to us. The strongest men will lay down and die if we ask them to. Police will arrest anyone we ask. Anything. Anything."

Ian Target stared at the small man who had appeared out of nowhere and immediately taken charge of the Consortium. He pursed his lips in thought.

"What are you thinking, Ian?" Veritas asked. "You're thinking that I'm in this just for myself? That I'm some sort of spoiled kid with a new toy? That this is just a game? That I will get tired of you and throw you away soon?"

Target grimaced. "Something like that." He paused and looked out the window. "There are a lot of good things that can be done for our cause with your abilities. If you were willing."

Veritas chuckled. "And what exactly is 'our cause'? I thought it was all about power." Veritas sighed. "Obviously, you want something. What is it?"

Target bit his lip. "Like I said, there are many things we can do together. But there is one good thing you can do for me. A gesture. Hard for me, easy for someone like you."

"What is it?"

"My sister," Target said. "Her name is Selah White. She's in prison in Texas on kidnapping charges. She has powers of her own. She could be a great asset to us, if…."

"If I were to get her set free," Veritas said. "I understand. Blood is thicker than water. All right, it's a deal. But first, tell me a little bit about the person who was responsible for putting her in prison. And I want to know more about these people that your Consortium is so eager to destroy. Heretics, I think you call them."

Before Target could answer, the cell phone in Veritas' coat pocket buzzed. He answered it.

"Yes," he said curtly. There was a pause, then he said, "Send them up." Another pause. "Yes, I understand. I don't care. Send them up anyway."

He put the phone away. "We're about to have visitors. Interpol."

Target's eyes widened, but Veritas held his hand up. "It'll be fine. Now tell me about this girl Constance Simeșcu. I understand that she's dating your son?"

"Was," Target said nervously, his mind still on the officers on their way up. "I sent him to the University of Texas to get close to her and find out what she knew. But then he decided to turn on me."

"Poor dad," Veritas said, chuckling. "Never understood, even when he foots the bill for his kid's education and their car. So you say they're not together anymore?"

Target shook his head. "From what I understand, no. I do think they're still friends, however."

At that point, the elevator opened, and five people stepped out. Four were uniformed officers with sidearms. The fifth was a suited woman who stepped forward and flashed an Interpol badge.

"Ian Target, you're under arrest for kidnapping and attempted murder," the woman said. "You'll be coming with us."

As Target watched, Veritas stepped forward and held out one hand, facing the five who entered the room. A familiar sweet smell began to permeate the air around them.

"Nonsense," he said. "Ian Target is a guest of mine. He'll be staying here. In fact, you don't think you found him when you came up here. Yes, he's left already. In fact, he's probably halfway to Japan by now."

Two of the policemen began to cough and one dropped his pistol. The woman stood blinking, her face slack, for a long moment. Suddenly she looked as if she had awakened from a dream.

"Now, was there anything else I could do for you?" Veritas asked her.

The Interpol officer blinked and looked at Veritas, as if confused.

"I'm sorry," she said. "I can't remember what we were doing here."

"You're all doing a wonderful job," Veritas said. "And I thank you for coming."

The officer who had dropped his pistol reached down and picked it up, putting it back in his holster. The Interpol woman nodded, and they all walked back to the elevator.

"That's impressive," Target said. "No matter how many times I see it happen."

"The trouble is, I have to be in the room with them to make it happen," Veritas said. "Which means I need to make a trip to Texas to visit your sister."

"It'll be good to see her again," Target said.

Veritas shook his head. "Oh, you're staying here. You're still a wanted man in America, and I have business you can take care of here. You can use this penthouse." He gestured around him.

"Now, tell me more about The Heretics and Constance Simeșcu."

* * *

Dr. Lane Murray Unit
Gatesville, Texas
48 Hours Later

Warden Hines Warren III considered himself a fair but tough man. As the warden of one of nine women's prisons in the Texas State Prison System, five of them in Gatesville, he had seen and heard all kinds of sob stories, witnessed all manner of nightmares, and could testify rightly that some of the women who were here were justly put behind bars, and some were not. He didn't really think about it, however. It wasn't his responsibility to decide guilt or innocence, thank goodness. That was taken care of by the court system, by the judges who listened to these stories every day and sometimes by juries as well. All Warden Warren had to do was make sure that the women who were declared guilty were locked up and served their sentences. He made sure they were safe while they were behind bars and others on the outside were safe from them.

For he knew that behind the most innocent, most beautiful face could be the most evil, malicious, dangerous mind conceivable. And while men might be stronger—*might*, mind you (he'd seen some incredibly strong women as well)—women made up for it in guile. And so twenty years as a prison warden taught him that guilty or innocent meant no difference to him. He treated them all the same.

There was one row of cells that the Unit kept for women who were exceptional troublemakers, those who couldn't get along with the others in general population or created problems for inmates or guards. Today there was only one prisoner there.

So it was that he was surprised when he got a call for an office visit regarding this prisoner. The guard outside his door opened it and let the slight man inside, who stepped forward and introduced himself.

"Thank you for meeting with me," the slight man said with a British accent. "I've just arrived from London, and I came right here."

"Well, what can I do for you, Mr. uh….?"

"Veritas," he said. "Just Veritas." He cleared his throat. "I've come to see about the release of Dr. Selah White."

Warden Warren sniffed the air, curiously, wondering where the strange, sweet smell was coming from. It was distracting.

"You're talking about a woman convicted of attempted murder and multiple counts of kidnapping," Warden Warren said. "I'll need to see a court order demanding her release before I can do anything."

Veritas smiled. "Oh, no you won't. In fact, you will draft up a paper claiming that she died in prison from a highly contagious form of something or other. That you buried her in the cemetery here. And then you will order your guards to bring her up here. And she and I will walk out of here, free. Isn't that right?"

The warden stared at Veritas for a long moment, before nodding slowly. He picked up his phone and pushed a button.

"Bruce, go down to Block A and bring back Prisoner 11327 named Selah White. She's in the isolation ward." He hung up the phone and looked back at Veritas.

"It will all be taken care of," he said.

8

The New World

South Chicago, Illinois

What am I doing here? Taupe thought. She dug her hands deeper into the pockets of her leather jacket and trudged down the streets of a city she swore she would never come back to, if ever she were able to escape it.

South Chicago. Home. Obviously, Harris Borden knew what he was doing when he gave her the envelope with instructions for her to go back to her own neighborhood. There were connections there she could use to get started, granted. But there was also a lot of bad influences and bad, bad memories. She looked down alleyways as she continued down the street, remembering that she got mugged in that alley, got high in that other alley, or perhaps almost raped in another alley.

Where to start? she wondered to herself. For years she had deferred to others in the group, always the one to complain, sure, willing to do the heavy lifting, but decision making? No thanks. And now, Harris had pushed the baby bird out of the nest. She had been around Harris, around Ruth and Josh for years, seeing them deliberate about how to best accomplish each mission while keeping everyone safe. What had she learned?

After close to a week here in Chicago, she had concluded that she needed to open herself up to God. In the beginning, she had felt that God wanted her to join the Heretics, to make a difference. And she had, and felt like she had helped make a difference more than once. But this was an opportunity to remember that when all was said and done, when all the organization and skills and equipment were taken away, it was simply a matter of being used by God for His will. Now all she needed to do was determine what that was.

And so she had been praying, probably more than she ever had in her life. She was alone, and there really wasn't anyone else to talk to. Several other people had tried to strike up conversations with her: a waitress, a truck driver, the guy at the front desk in the seedy hotel where she was staying. But she stayed focused on hearing God's voice. Could God have spoken through those other people? Probably, but she didn't get the sense that was where God was leading her.

Now she was walking back to her old haunts, wondering what had happened to the kids she went to high school with: who had lived, who had died, and who had gotten out of the neighborhood. She stopped when she came to a street sign. It read: Look Street. Someone had crossed out Street and written "Ahead" beneath it. The sign struck her strangely, and she looked at what was more of an alley than a street. There was no more indication that the street was any different than any of the others she had passed, but she decided to turn into the alley.

The notorious Chicago wind, coming right off Lake Michigan, was biting cold, and the alley gave her some comfort from the frigid weather. She moved deeper into the alleyway and saw steam blowing out of pipes from buildings on either side of the alley. Most homeless people that she knew, this being January, tried to find spaces at the several shelters in the area, especially when it was cold like this. It was very dangerous to be homeless in the winter in Chicago, and she remembered from her street days how often the police would find homeless people frozen to death in the early morning hours.

As she thought about it, she got the chilling feeling that she would find the same thing this morning. Sure enough, she saw the body of a young Black woman, lying beneath a steam outlet on a stack of cardboard with a coat thrown over her. She went over to check on her and realized that the young woman was about her same age. She rolled her over and realized that she was someone she knew.

"Stephanie," she said to the unconscious woman. "Stephanie, are you okay?" She felt her throat and saw that there was a faint pulse there.

"Stephanie, it's me, Rosetta," Taupe said. She cringed as she used her real name, a name she hadn't used for many years, probably not since high school. "Stephanie, wake up."

Finally, Stephanie began to moan and move around.

"I'm so cold," Stephanie muttered weakly. She pulled her coat over her and tried to roll over to go back to sleep.

"Stephanie, you're laying in an alley in the winter in Chicago. Of course, you're cold. I need to call an ambulance for you."

Stephanie shook her head. "No amblulance," she slurred. "No cops."

"Stephanie, I'm not a doctor, but you might have hypothermia," Taupe said. Stephanie rolled over again and closed her eyes. Taupe pulled out her burner cell phone and dialed 911.

"I know you'll be mad at me for this, Stephanie," Taupe said. "But it's for your own good."

* * *

East Los Angeles

Children of God Mission: God Loves You and So Do We

Josh stood on the street outside the old, boarded-up building that used to be one of several around the country serving the needy. He hadn't been to this one before, but the one in Seattle had played a major part in bringing him and Ruth in as homeless teens, and eventually linking them up with Harris Borden.

He smiled as he thought back to those days, how naïve they were, how convicted they were in their beliefs and how much they trusted Harris. He then frowned as he saw what had happened to the mission here, wondering if the same thing had happened at all the other missions.

He saw a couple of Hispanic teens working on a car a couple of doors down from the mission and walked down to talk to them.

"*Hola,*" he said to them. "*¿Cuándo cerró la misión?*"

The two teens stared at him blankly. "What do you need, sir?" one of them finally asked.

"Oh, sorry," Josh said. "I was just wondering when the mission shut down."

One of them shrugged. "It's been closed down for at least ten years. Maybe more."

Josh frowned. "Do either one of you know a guy name Rico? Likes to fix cars? He's a Christian? Has gang tattoos on his arms?"

The two teens looked at each other blankly and shook their heads.

"You're probably thinking of Pastor Escobar," Josh heard from the front steps of the house where they were working. He turned and saw a man in his forties, standing in a T-shirt and a beer in his hand. He had a Ronin tattoo on his shoulder and a beer belly beginning to show.

"*Pastor* Escobar?" Josh echoed.

The man laughed. "Yeah, goes by Richard now. Makes his congregation more comfortable. He went mainstream. He has a church over in West Hollywood. Why do you want him?"

"I was told to look him up by someone he knew a long time ago," Josh said. "Elijah Brown."

The man whistled. "Not sure what kind of reception you're going to get with that name. Rico's made himself comfortable now. Got a pretty wife, a big church. Not sure he'll want to be reminded of his past." He took a sip of his beer, then chuckled. "Of course, it might be just the thing he needs."

* * *

Georgetown, Maryland
Outside Washington, D.C.

The sign on the front door of the office was nondescript, just as Douglas and Ruth intended it to be. The black-on-white business cards that Douglas handed out in his face-to-face conversations simply read: Center for Concerned Studies, followed by a phone number. There was no street or mailing address, and no name was associated with it. That is the way they wanted to keep it, mostly for their own safety, both considering what they were doing and what had happened with the Heretics recently.

Ruth took care of the office and online responsibilities, while Douglas connected with individuals on the Hill. He was very careful who he talked to about what he was doing and what his intentions were. Their plan was to simply start gathering up and organizing information that could be used by someone in power—law enforcement, Justice Department, Senate investigations committee—who might be interested in proof of corruption in the federal government. Both Ruth and Douglas believed that eventually they would be contacted by Sparky, the government source that officially was anonymous but which they had traced back to Senator Albert Bemis. At that time, they would know more where all of this was leading.

They were in their office about a week before the phone call came. Douglas was just about to leave for another day of visiting congressional aides and secretaries when the desk phone rang. It was the first time that either of them had heard it ring, and at first, they stared at it in disbelief.

"Maybe it's a wrong number," Ruth said, staring at the phone.

"Maybe," Douglas said, skeptical. He reached for it and answered.

"Center for Concerned Studies," he said cautiously.

"Well, I see you two have finally gotten settled," the voice said. "Glad to see that you are making some connections. And I even like the name. Center for Concerned Studies." The voice laughed. "I don't think I can imagine a more generic title than that. Good for you."

"I assume this is Sparky I'm talking to?" Douglas said.

"The one and only," Sparky said. "I'm calling to see if you two need anything."

"A little direction would be helpful," Douglas said. "Right now, we feel we're wandering through a dark storm drain without a flashlight."

"I don't think you need that much direction," Sparky said. "I know you, and I know what kind of congressman you were. Resourceful. Honorable. Tenacious. Just stay with the task. Talk to people. Mingle. Get invited to parties. And then keep good records."

"And then what?" Douglas said. "Do I turn it over to the Justice Department?"

"No," the voice said. "Keep digging and you'll see why not. I'll be in touch soon enough. Then we'll act on it. You'll hear from me soon."

Sparky hung up the phone and Douglas held the receiver for a long moment before he put it down slowly. Ruth saw the puzzled look on his face.

"Well?" she said. "What did you learn?"

Douglas told her everything that Sparky had said on the phone call. Ruth shook her head.

"I don't feel very comfortable with this situation," Ruth said. "We're deep undercover, and we don't even know the name of our contact person. Not really. Are you sure we're doing the right thing?"

Douglas frowned. "Look, we're looking for corruption in all its forms in the federal government. All we are doing is keeping records of our detective work. We're not arresting anyone. What are we doing wrong?"

Ruth shook her head. "I don't know. It all seems very wrong to me." She paused. "Look, you keep doing what you need to do. Hobnob with the Hill People. I'm going to try to connect with Bobby and see what I can find out about Sparky. You okay with that?"

Douglas nodded. "Just be careful, okay?" He reached for his jacket and put it on. "I will try to get us invited to a few dinners. I'm not a congressman anymore, but I still know a few people, including some lobbyists who owe me."

Ruth sighed. "Guess I need to take our formal wear to the drycleaners." She leaned forward and kissed Douglas, who then went out the front door of the office and was gone.

Ruth immediately got on her burner phone and texted Harris Borden, her only contact with Bobby: **Need B.**

Kiev, Ukraine

It was late afternoon in Europe when Harris Borden got the text from Ruth: **Need B**. Harris was sitting on a small balcony drinking tea while overlooking the city square with St. Sophia's Cathedral on the other side. Curious, he thought it was time he checked up on Ruth and Douglas. He decided to risk it and made a Facetime call to Ruth. It buzzed twice, and Ruth answered.

"Harris," Ruth said, smiling. "It's good to see your face."

"It's good to see yours," Harris said, smiling back. "I know this is somewhat of a risk, but I missed everyone. We'll make this a quick call. How is everything going?"

Ruth shrugged. "We have an office and business cards. Douglas is making some connections. That's about as far as we've gotten. Oh, and we just got a really creepy call from our contact, Sparky."

"Sparky, huh?" Harris said. "Is that why you need B?"

Ruth nodded. "Better safe than sorry. I'm probably being paranoid, I know."

"No such thing as paranoid in our game, Sweetheart," Harris said. "I'll have him contact you. Stay safe. Remember to trash that burner phone."

Harris switched off the call and then called Bobby on Facetime as well. The phone rang several times before Bobby answered. He looked a little bleary eyed.

"Oh, hey Boss," Bobby said. "How's Ukraine?"

"How did you know I was in Ukraine?" Harris said, surprised.

Bobby laughed. "You have St. Sophia's Cathedral in the distance there. I've always wanted to go there." He rubbed his eyes. "Sorry, I'm not at my sharpest this morning. We're at the Grand Canyon and we stayed up late last night driving to get to the park."

Harris laughed. "You and Peewee enjoying yourselves?"

Bobby nodded. "But of course, it's not all fun and games. I've been doing some research. I found out a little bit about these teams that hit our trainees. Someone from Europe—either French, Italian or Hungarian—was responsible for leaking their itinerary to the hit squads. I will need to get a list of the delegations that were at your meeting in Salzburg to determine more."

"I can get that list for you," Harris said. "Is there any indication who sent out the hit teams?"

"I started by tracing our friend Ian Target. He joined up with a group called the Consortium in the U.K. shortly before all this happened," Bobby said, speaking as he looked at notes on his screen. "They had a meeting in Scotland a few weeks ago, and right after that was when we got hit. So put two and two together...."

"Chances are, they're the ones behind this," Harris said. "What do we know about the Consortium?"

"What I can tell is they are a group of power broker billionaires that meet once each year somewhere in the world," Bobby said. "They used to go by the name 'Brotherhood of the Altar.'"

Harris nodded to himself. "Yeah, they and I go way back. The first time I crashed a Brotherhood meeting I was thrown off a rooftop."

Bobby whistled. "They realized early on how much power they had and decided to pool that power to have even more influence."

"That's never a good thing," Harris muttered. "Okay, you're doing good. Just don't get caught. It sounds like they could be dangerous to cross, so we need to be very careful."

"Oh, I'm always careful, Boss," Bobby said. "Was there something else?"

"Ruth called me. She and Douglas are in D.C. working for some guy named Sparky who wants them to investigate corruption in the federal government," Harris said, a suspicious tone in his voice.

"And he's called Sparky because...?"

"Well, he's anonymous," Harris said. "I can give you Ruth's office number. Sparky called them today. See what you can find out about him. Better to be safe than sorry."

"Got it, Boss," Bobby said. "I'll do what I can."

"You and Pee Wee stay safe," Harris said to Bobby.

"You too, Harris. I'll get that info to you ASAP."

They both hung up. Harris sat for a long moment and savored the view before getting up. He knew when he made the call that he would have to check out and move again, lest those who were after them would catch up.

He folded up his laptop and went inside to pack. 𝒱

9

Fools for Christ

Connie didn't really know what to expect when she got back to classes the next Monday. She had a lot of catching up to do—it seemed like catching up was the story of her life—and she felt like she needed to focus on something she could do well, like school. But her father's heart attack, followed by the guilt associated with leaving him to follow what she thought was God's leading here in Austin weighed down on her. She had hoped to find some solace in talking to Josh or even Taupe, but when she arrived, they were nowhere to be found. Not even Prof. Washington was in his office. And so the weighted-down feeling became a heavy depression.

It's just Satan trying to crush your spirit, she told herself. Knowing this, she got up extra early and started her day by reading The Beatitudes in Matthew 5. She read through them several times, a passage she already knew almost by heart, and the words kept flowing through her mind as she walked the hallways of UT.

"Blessed are the poor in spirit, for theirs is the kingdom of heaven. Blessed are those who mourn, for they will be comforted."

Today was her first day in the new Philosophy of Life course that Prof. Valencia—*Rico Suavé*—encouraged her to take. The discussion was different, and she was lost at first, but soon she found it interesting. As the class was just about to end, Valencia looked at her and nodded.

"I didn't want to embarrass her earlier, but we have a new student in class," he said. "Connie Simescu has joined the class on my invitation, and I've invited her to be one of the speakers for our end of the semester seminar. That is, if she's willing."

Connie nodded. "I've prayed about it, and I think I can do this," she said. "Can you say a little more about it?"

"We'll be having a planning session in a few weeks to meet with the three speakers. We'll tell you more then." He looked at the rest of the class. "As you all know, the seminar is entitled, 'Science, Magic, or Faith,' and we have been looking for someone willing to represent the faith portion of our presentation." He smiled at Connie. "Although Connie and I may not share the same convictions when it comes to God, I respect her viewpoint and her ability to share that. I look forward to a stimulating discussion."

Connie felt her face flush as other students looked at her, some frowning, some laughing quietly.

"Blessed are you when people insult you, persecute you and falsely say all kinds of evil against you because of me."

Connie was thinking of that line from the Beatitudes as she left the class, and she heard a small group of students standing outside the classroom.

"Hey Connie," a tall blonde guy shouted as she left. "Better pray real hard before that seminar. That crowd is going to eat you alive." The others began to laugh as she walked away.

"Who knows," a girl said, laughing. "Maybe Jesus will save her."

What have I done? Connie asked herself, thinking about the seminar. *They don't want to hear what I believe. They just want to tear me apart, like Christians in the arena with lions. I'm fooling myself.*

"We are fools for Christ, but you are so wise in Christ! We are weak, but you are strong! You are honored, we are dishonored!" The words from I Corinthians 4:10 came to her mind.

This was what she had left her parents for. To follow God into the unknown land. To be a fool for Christ. Humiliated. Ignored. Perhaps beaten. Maybe even killed. She thought she was brave, but now she knew she was not. This is what The Messenger talked about. Was she able to go ahead, possibly all alone?

She looked ahead of her in the empty hallway, and there stood Marita. For a moment, she almost thought that she was imagining her former best friend. Marita stood quietly, wearing her usual blue skirt and red sweater, staring at her. She smiled at Connie, the same smile that Connie remembered from so many times before, a smile of recognition. A warm, welcoming smile. And then she turned and stepped out a doorway.

"Wait!" Connie called after her. "Wait, Marita! I want to talk to you!" She ran down the empty hallway to the door where Marita had disappeared. The parking lot beyond was empty.

Connie's heart sunk. She fell against the wall inside the doorway and stared out into the street where Marita had disappeared.

"I can't do this," she whispered to God. "Not alone. Please, God. Please give me direction. Please give me a sign. Please send me someone to work with me."

She stood there, leaning against the wall, praying silently for guidance, some kind of sign for a long while, but none came. She was alone in Austin.

Sure, Adam was still around, she thought. But Connie saw him as pretty much worthless. He didn't commit to anything or anyone. He didn't want to be in charge of anything, and now he'd dropped out of school. She told people that they had broken up because he kept flirting with other girls, but deep down, Connie wondered if it was because she was a lot more focused in her life, and Adam still seemed to be floating in his. All his life his father, the billionaire Ian Target, had taken care of him. And in two years, Adam would inherit a trust fund worth millions. That most likely contributed to Adam's lack of direction, Connie thought. All he had to do was wait two years and he wouldn't have to work a day in his life.

The only thing Adam took seriously was working at Josh's bookstore. For some reason, Connie saw that Adam found himself at home when he worked there. Connie wondered what would happen to Adam now that Josh was no longer around.

Nope, she couldn't babysit Adam anymore. There were too many important things to do.

"Time to suck it up, Con-con," Connie muttered to herself. She bit her lip and stepped out the door and into the parking lot. Her classes were done for the day and she had to choose between going back to the bookstore or the dorm. Usually on Mondays she would go over to Taupe's dojo and hang out, but that wouldn't happen anymore. And she felt odd going over to the bookstore without Josh there.

She thought about people she'd known before. She was tempted to call Ezra Huddleston, Maddie's fiancé, but with things the way they were with Maddie, she didn't think that was a good idea. Plus, she had already gotten Ezra into trouble once.

She thought of Harold Innsmuir, the editor of the *Austin Times*, who had given her an internship the year before. He had really wanted to hire her as a reporter, but times were tough for newspapers, and when she saw how things were struggling, she decided to not pursue journalism as a career. Since that time, they hadn't had much contact.

Then she thought of Bill Hall, the owner of The Roadhouse, the restaurant/bar/club where she and Marita had worked when she first came to Austin. She missed Bill and Luther, the bartender. In addition, she realized that she really needed a new job. With her internship gone and Josh disappeared, money would dry up quickly. In addition, there was always the possibility that Marita had come back there to work, and she would find another connection with her.

It was a long way over to Sixth Street, but she caught the local bus and headed over there. She wanted to get to The Roadhouse before things got busy in the evening, and she was lucky to arrive around four. As usual, Bill was in the back, stocking shelves.

"Hi Bill," Connie said, awkwardly.

"Connie!" Bill said, stepping toward her and wrapping her in a hug. "How are you? What's the language count these days?"

"Uh, I just added Mandarin, so I think that makes twelve that I'm fluent in. About another eight I'm working on."

Bill shook his head. "You're a genius, you know that?"

"Being a genius doesn't pay the bills," Connie said wryly. "I'm looking for work."

Bill looked at her and frowned. "Well, we have plenty of waitstaff right now, but you've got a reliable record with us. And your ability with languages always comes in handy here on Sixth Street." He looked around him. "Tell you what. I need some help back here with stocking, with keeping books and loading and unloading. Think you can do that? Then when a server opening comes up, you'll be first in line."

Connie frowned, then nodded. "The tips were always what made the job worthwhile here." She brightened. "That and the company. Sure. I can do odds and ends until something better comes."

"Okay, I am pretty much set for today," Bill said. "See if Luther needs anything."

She went out front to the bar where Luther was stocking his liquor for the evening under the cabinets. "Hey, Luther," she said. "Is there anything I can help you with out here?"

Luther grinned and threw her a cloth and some disinfectant spray.

"Sure, you can spray everything down and wipe it clean," he said. "The bar, the tables and chairs, everything. I try to do it once at the beginning of the night and if I get a chance a couple more times per night, but you know how busy it gets around here. How are you doing these days?"

Connie shrugged. "Oh, you know. My dad just had a heart attack and my friends all left town. I'm muddling through."

Luther shook his head. "Sorry to hear that. Glad you're back with us. I like your jacket, by the way."

"Thanks," Connie said, looking at her denim jacket and smiling slightly, but thinking about her father.

She helped for another hour or so, and then business started picking up at The Roadhouse, and she found herself in the way, so she excused herself. She walked down Sixth Street toward the campus in the early evening hours. It was too late for the afternoon tourists, and still too early for the evening club crowd, so things were somewhat quiet. She decided to walk back to campus rather than taking the bus.

She went down an alley to cut past the busiest part of Sixth Street and got her closest to Guadalupe Avenue, where she would head north. When she did, she though she noticed some movement above her on the tops of the old buildings. She didn't actually see anything, but it was more like a blur. Frowning, she thrust her hands in her pockets and walked faster down the alley, looking at the ground all the way.

A few steps later, some gravel rattled down from the building on the other side. Connie paused and looked up, caught between a sense of fear and curiosity. She stood there watching for a long moment before she sighed and stepped out onto the main street.

This time she kept her peripheral vision aware and realized that someone was following her. As she walked, she didn't really see him, but she could sense his presence. Small noises, a few rocks falling here, a scuffling sound there, would tell her that someone unseen was following her.

Someone was on the rooftops, she realized suddenly, *and that someone was following her.* The hair stood up on her neck. *What should she do?*

She came around a corner and saw a police cruiser parked on the corner. One of the officers was inside on the radio, and the other stood outside the passenger door, looking up.

"Did you see anyone up there? On the rooftops?" the officer asked her as she approached in the evening light.

She shook her head. "No, but I heard him." She turned and looked back in the direction she had come. Suddenly she saw a reflection in the window of an apartment building. "There," she pointed.

A figure in a dark hoodie leaped from the edge of the tall building and soared across the alley between buildings. For a moment, it looked like the person would make it across the chasm, but the distance was just a little too far. The dark, hooded figure caught the edge of the next building and hung there for a long moment, then fell to a fire escape just below it.

In the meantime, the officer that Connie was speaking to ran toward the hooded figure, who Connie could see was a Black adolescent boy. The boy had collapsed into a heap on the fire escape, then picked himself up. When he saw the officer running toward him, followed by Connie and the other officer who had gotten out of the cruiser, he got up and started to run, but Connie saw that he was limping. The boy wore a Spiderman T-shirt and had bright orange hair.

"Hold it right there," the first officer said to him, placing his hand on his sidearm. The boy started to run, but realized that he wouldn't get far, and held up his hands in surrender. The officer climbed the fire escape and pulled a pair of handcuffs out and proceeded to put them on the teenager.

"Wait," Connie said. "You're not arresting him, are you? You're not even going to check to see if he's okay? What did he do that was against the law?"

The officers chuckled to each other. "You saw what we saw. Reckless endangerment. Trespassing. And we've gotten reports of a 10-14 in the area."

"What's a 10-14?" Connie asked.

"It's a prowler, and I'm not one," the kid said. "I'm just learning parkour."

"What's parkour?"

"It's an extreme sport that calls for people to jump from tall buildings and risk their necks," the other officer said. "There's a rash of that going around Austin. Too many people getting injured that way."

"Look, did you arrest those other people?" Connie asked. "He said he's not a prowler, and he wasn't hurting anyone else."

"Didn't you see him?" the first officer said. "He was about to break his neck."

"Yeah, well it's my neck to break, isn't it?" the boy said.

"Son, someone needs to teach you some manners," the first officer said. "Especially when it comes to the police."

"Listen, he's just a kid," Connie said. "How about I take responsibility for him?"

"Who are you?"

"I'm Connie Simescu," she said. "I was the girl kidnapped a couple of months ago. It was in the news. Detective Lee Shapiro can vouch for me."

"So why should we leave him with you?" the first officer said.

87

"Look, she's right," the second officer said to his partner. "We got enough to deal with. Let her worry about the kid."

The first officer looked at Connie, then the boy, then at his partner and shrugged.

"Okay, it's your funeral," the officer said. "But if he gets into trouble, I'll have Shapiro look you up." The officer unlocked the handcuffs and looked the kid in the eye.

"Stay off the rooftops, you hear me?"

The boy didn't reply but grinned as the two officers left.

"Are you okay?" Connie asked, reaching for the boy. He flinched and pulled away.

"What's your name, kid?" Connie asked.

"Trash," the kid said.

"What was that?" Connie said. "Trask? Is that your name?"

"No," he said. "Trash. I go by Trash."

"I'm not calling you that," Connie said. "What does your mama call you?"

The boy got quiet. "Rupert," he muttered.

Connie scrunched up her nose. "Well, I see why you'd want to change your name, but Trash won't do. We'll have to look for another name for you. You look about eleven."

"I'm thirteen."

"Where do you live?"

Trash shrugged. "Mama died last year. I make do."

"You in school?"

"I was," Trash muttered. "Not anymore. Looking for adventure."

"How? By jumping off buildings?"

"Sure, why not," Trash said. "What's this world got to offer me anyway?"

Like a bolt of lightning, it suddenly struck Connie that this was the kid that she had seen in her dream who had muttered: *"I'm waiting for you to save me."*

"Well, as far as this world is concerned, you're probably right," Connie said. "They don't have a lot to offer you. But I hang with some people who have a lot more for you than you can imagine. Do you believe in Jesus?"

Trash nodded. "Sure do. But the white Jesus that my church talks about is too tame. They wants us to be meek and mild. I follow the Black Jesus and he has a different path for me. The man is dope."

"Trash," Connie said, cringing as she said the name. "You *have* to meet my friends. You're going to fit right in." 🜨

10

Miracle the Dog

West Hollywood

The church wasn't huge compared to some of the mega-churches that Josh had been in over the years, but the West Hills Congregational Church featured about 5,000 members as far as he saw that morning. And considering where their pastor, Rico (now Richard) Escobar started, this church was a very large step up for him.

Deacons stood by the doorways with very large baskets collecting offering as people exited the church service, and the baskets were getting filled to overflowing. The people who lined up to leave were dressed as if they were attending the ballet or opera, most of them in fine suits and furs, white and middle aged. The huge sanctuary was lined with red cedar paneling, and brass was everywhere, brightly serving as either stair railing or posts for the red sashes that controlled traffic flow. As Josh looked around, he saw few people of color in the congregation and raised his eyebrow, wondering how in the world an ex-gang member from the barrio could become a pastor for this crowd.

He watched the young Pastor Escobar from a distance, milling through the crowd, shaking hands and slapping shoulders, smiling behind his tinted glasses, the tattoos that Josh knew were on his arms carefully hidden by the long sleeves of his expensive Brooks Brothers suit. Finally, Josh decided that he had seen enough, and stepped forward. When Pastor Escobar saw Josh coming, the 30-something man in casual slacks and a dress shirt with a burn scar covering one side of his face, Josh saw a moment's hesitation. But Pastor Escobar recovered quickly and reached forward to shake Josh's hand.

"Welcome to our church," he said. "I don't think we've met."

"We haven't," Josh said. "My name is Josh. I do believe we know someone in common. Elijah Brown?"

Josh watched Pastor Escobar's eyes carefully and saw a twitch hit them when he mentioned the name that Harris Borden had gone by for many years. He was Elijah Brown when he was in hiding from the law and establishing his support of Christian believers in underdeveloped parts of cities across the U.S. Those believers would become the foundation for both the Heretics and the Children of God missions, the fate of which Josh was still trying to discover.

"Now that's a name I haven't heard in a very long time," Pastor Escobar said quietly. He looked up at the exiting parishioners, then at the deacons. He gestured at one of them. "Peter, take over for me, please?" He looked back at Josh and tipped his head as a gesture for him to follow him.

Josh followed him down the long aisle with the rich red carpet to the front of the sanctuary, all the while looking at the beautiful colored light that streamed in through stained glass on all sides. When Pastor Escobar saw that Josh had slowed, he turned to him.

"Beautiful, isn't it?" Pastor Escobar said. "This place was a dump before I got here and started motivating our members to support its renovation. Last year we completed our building project. Five years and twenty million dollars. Can you believe it?"

They went through double doors and down another hallway until they came to what looked like an office. Josh suspected it was an office, although the outside simply said, "Private." Pastor Escobar reached into his pocket and fished out a ring of keys to quickly unlock the door. Inside was a very small, very modest office with a small desk.

"I have a larger office on the other side of the church, with a mahogany desk and all the trappings," Pastor Escobar said. "But this is where I started, and this is where I come to pray. In fact, I think God can hear me better here than in that other place. That's more for show. This is where I work."

"Do your parishioners know who you are and where you come from?"

Pastor Escobar smiled faintly. "A few. This place was looking for a spark. I was looking for a way out. It just worked out that we could help each other."

Josh looked back behind him. "Seems like a lot of this church is built for show."

The smile left Pastor Escobar's face, and he was obviously offended. He tipped his head.

"I know that the people here aren't what we're used to," Pastor Escobar said. "They're not Children of God class people. But they need God too. And they can do a lot of good with just a little direction."

"Like spending $20 million on themselves while the Children of God Mission closes its doors?" Josh said. "Or did you know about that?"

Pastor Escobar nodded sadly. "That happened a while back. I tried to get the church to support what was going on there, but there were other priorities that took precedence here."

"Yeah, like stained glass and plush carpet," Josh said. "How many people did the Children of God help back in the day? Or do you remember? And how many are they helping now?"

Pastor Escobar pursed his lips and looked at the floor. "You're not telling me anything I didn't already know." He looked up. "If I know Elijah Brown, he didn't send you here just to prick my conscience. What are you here for?"

A slow smile crept across Josh's face. "Call it Project Lazarus. We're about to resurrect the dead."

Pastor Escobar nodded slowly. "I'm listening," he said.

* * *

Austin, Texas

Connie and Trash walked/limped—Connie walked, he limped—the rest of the way over to Guadalupe Street and the bookstore.

Connie told Trash briefly about the Heretics on the way there. Trash was skeptical the entire way, but Connie realized that Trash had gone through a lot in the last few years, so skepticism may have become his way of life. She tried to see through his scowling face. *Give him time,* she felt rather than heard inside her.

They decided to cut through an alley that led to Guadalupe just a few blocks from the bookstore. It was about an hour after dark and the shadows were deep everywhere. Connie was normally a bit nervous about walking through alleys, especially at night, but this was one she had traversed a million times, and so she didn't think anything of it. What caught her by surprise was the pickup parked at the entrance with a man outside the cab hunched over a burlap sack on the ground. He was beating it with a stick, and howls and cries of pain were coming from the sack.

Connie paused for a second, not sure what she was seeing. Then she stepped forward.

"Hey," she said. "What are you doing? Stop it."

"Mind your own business," the man said, and she realized that he was drunk. "It's just a mangy mutt. Bit me one time too many. I'm going to show him."

"No, you aren't," came from above him. Connie realized that Trash wasn't at her side anymore. She looked up to see him standing on a nearby fire escape above their heads. As the drunken man raised the stick one more time, Trash threw a can at the man, hitting him in the shoulder.

"Hey," the man said, turning toward Trash. "Hey kid. Stop that. Come down here and let me teach you something." The man took two steps toward Trash, and Connie realized that the man was way too drunk to climb the fire escape. Of course, he still planned to get back into his truck and drive away, which would be dangerous for other people.

"Hey, Mister," Connie said. "You shouldn't be driving."

"Buzz off, Sister," the man said over his shoulder. He started to turn toward her, then Trash threw another can and hit the man in the

93

chest. The man hesitated, then lumbered toward Trash like a drunken Godzilla.

"Now," Trash shouted at Connie.

"Now?" Connie said, not sure what he was thinking of.

Trash gestured at the burlap sack, still lying on the pavement, and indicated that she should carry it away. Connie finally realized what he was suggesting, as the man finally reached the foot of the fire escape. She started to do as Trash suggested, then realized that something else was important here, and she ran over to the cab of the man's pickup and reached inside.

"Come on down here, you little creep," the man said. "I'm gonna plaster you."

"Hey Mister," she said to him, and he turned. Connie held up his keys.

"Come by the Reborn Bookstore on Guadalupe when you are sober, and you can get your keys back." She then lifted the heavy sack and started running down the alley toward the bookstore.

"Give me back my keys!" the man shouted after her. He took a few steps in her direction, then remembered that he had a teenage boy treed above him on the fire escape. He turned to attack the boy again and realized that the boy had left in the meantime.

"NOOOOOO!" the man shouted.

Connie ran as far as she could, the dog inside the sack squirming in her arms. It was heavy, and she was tempted to stop and let it out, but she didn't dare stop before she got out of the range of the drunken man who had been beating the dog. After she left the alley, she found herself on Guadalupe Street, just a couple of blocks away from the bookstore. Even so, she had to put the sack down on the sidewalk and catch her breath.

"Here," she heard behind her, and Trash came running up. He grabbed the sack and lifted it up, with a slight yelp coming from the inside of the sack. "Shall we open it?"

"Not until we get him inside the bookstore," Connie said. "Who knows what kinds of wounds we'll be dealing with. And it's always dangerous to treat a wounded animal, especially one that's been mistreated by humans like this. We're going to need Adam's help." She headed down the street, and Trash carried the sack.

"Who's Adam?"

"A friend," Connie said. "You'll meet him soon enough."

"You mean like boyfriend, friend?"

Connie grinned. "Sort of. Used to be. You'll meet him."

A few minutes later, they were outside the front entrance to the Reborn Bookstore. It was past seven, and Connie knew that Adam liked to close shop about then. Business had been off since Josh had disappeared, even with Adam's superb coffee brewing, and so they had cut back the evening business hours. They saw that Adam had already locked the front door when they got there, and so Connie rapped on the glass. A moment later, Adam, dressed in a cardigan sweater, opened the door.

"About time you showed up," Adam said. "I've discovered something." Connie pushed past him into the store, followed by Trash, carrying the burlap sack. "Who's he? What's that in your hands?"

"We rescued a dog," Trash said. "Connie said you would know what to do."

Adam's eyebrows raised and he looked at Connie. "What made you think I'd know what to do? Do I look like a vet?"

"A drunk was beating the dog with a stick," Connie said. "We had to do something."

Adam sighed. "Okay, let's take him up to Josh's apartment. We'll open up the bag and see what we have up there." Connie grinned back at him and hugged Adam. Adam looked skeptical at Trash. "You still haven't told me who this is."

Trash stepped forward. "My name is——."

"His name is *Crash*," Connie said, interrupting. "He's a parkour champion. He's really good."

She looked at Trash/Crash with an eyebrow raised, who hesitated, then nodded at the name change.

"Crash, huh?" Adam said, looking at the kid skeptically. "I'm sure there's a story there." He turned to Connie. "Come on, let's get the dog upstairs."

The three of them took the sack upstairs, with Connie making sure they handled it as carefully as possible. When they got inside Josh's apartment, they lay it down in the middle of the room and Adam slowly untied the opening of the sack.

"Dogs don't do well when they've been mistreated, even when they have been rescued by strangers," Adam said. "We may have to give him a little space. And a little time."

Connie nodded. "I understand. I already have a name for him. Miracle. He's a miracle to have survived all of this."

"It'll be a miracle if we don't all get bit," Crash muttered. "How do you know it's a 'him'?"

Adam didn't respond but opened the bag. He pulled the top back slowly and then stepped back.

Inside was a Rottweiler puppy, about four months old. It was a male, just as Connie had suspected. He looked bruised and dazed, and at first, he pulled back from the three humans. Then he started to growl. Then whine.

"Easy, Miracle," Connie said to the dog. "We don't want to hurt you." She turned to Crash. "Can you find him a bowl and get him some water?"

"I don't see any blood," Adam said. "Consider what you described, that's a miracle in itself."

"He looks starved to death." She paused, then looked at Adam. "You said you discovered something," Connie said. "Something you wanted to share with me."

"It can wait," Adam said. "I thought I'd made some progress on Josh's computer. I got past the computer password, but he has his hard drive encrypted. I'll need to hack that too."

Connie sighed. "Well, keep working on it."

Crash brought the water, and Miracle stopped growling long enough to drink the entire bowl of water, most of it splashing all over the floor.

"I'll get him some more," Adam said. "Then I suggest we let him get some sleep up here tonight. We don't know what other injuries he has."

"You going to let that dog loose in this apartment?" Crash asked.

"You're going to stay here and keep an eye on him," Connie said to Crash. Then she turned to Adam. "Adam, Crash needs a place to stay."

"Of course," Adam responded, sighing.

Connie reached forward and petted Miracle's head. The dog flinched, then let her touch him.

"Miracle, we are going to leave you here tonight," she said. "Tomorrow morning I'll bring back some dog food and feed you. But tonight, I'll make you a nice, soft bed. But you need to promise me you won't tear up Josh's apartment. Okay?"

Miracle responded by shaking his head, with water spraying everywhere.

"Oh, I can tell this is going to work out just great," Adam said wryly, wiping himself off.

"How much dog food do you think a rottweiler puppy eats?" Connie asked.

"More than you can afford," Adam said. "More than all of us can afford."

An hour later, Connie had left the bookstore, Miracle and Crash had settled in on the sofa upstairs and Adam realized that he hadn't finished shutting things down downstairs. He went down the stairs and began shutting off lights. When he got to the front desk, he realized that the trash needed emptying and the coffee pot still needed washing out if it were to be ready for tomorrow morning. He took the coffee maker to the sink in the back of the bookstore and rinsed it out, put a little detergent in it and scrubbed it, then rinsed it again. He dried it and put it by the sink. Then he went back to the front desk and picked up the trash can there. He visited two other locations in the bookstore with trash cans and emptied them out in the can. Then he carried the can out to the back entrance of the bookstore where the dumpster was located.

It was not quite nine o'clock, and he could hear traffic and people talking, laughing, and shouting on Guadalupe Street on the other side of the building. Six months before, Adam would have thought it was time to go out and find some place to party. But despite Connie not taking him seriously, he had changed in the past six months. He wasn't ready to be in charge; he'd be the first to admit that. But he realized by hanging around with Harris Borden, Josh, and the Heretics that life was about more than having a good time.

He dumped the trash can into the dumpster and turned to go back into the bookstore when a lone figure stepped out of the shadows. It was a small, slight man, dressed in an overcoat, with a suit beneath it. In fact, he was dressed unlike anyone Adam had seen here in Texas. And then Adam realized that the man was dressed very similar to the men that his own father, Ian Target, often associated with.

"Pardon me," the man said, and Adam immediately caught a British accent. "I'm looking for the Reborn Bookstore. Is this it?"

Adam looked at the man, then back at the closed door that led to the bookstore.

"Well, you found it, but we're closed," Adam said. "We close at seven."

"I see," the man said. "Pity. Would you happen to be Joshua Brown?"

Adam shook his head. "'Fraid not. Josh is out of town. I'm his assistant, Adam Target. Is there something I can help you with?"

The man stepped forward and held out his hand. Adam saw that he wore expensive leather gloves.

"Let me introduce myself," he said. "Anais Singleton. I have a confession to share. I'm not here to talk to him about the bookstore. I am here to talk to him about Elijah Brown and the Heretics." The man paused. "I'm sorry. Are you acquainted with…Elijah Brown?"

Adam hesitated. Who was this man, and how much should he tell him?

"I'm here to ask for their help," Singleton said. He stood there, still holding his hand out to be shaken by Adam. Finally, Adam stepped forward and took the man's hand and shook it.

"Well, I don't know a lot, but what I do know I can share with you. Why don't you come on in? Would you like a cup of coffee? We have great coffee here."

Singleton smiled thinly and nodded. "Thank you very much."

As they stepped into the bookstore, a sickly sweet aroma began to follow them into the room. 𝒱

11

Food for All

Chicago South Hospital
Chicago, Illinois

The med-surg wing of Chicago South Hospital was busy, and typically the nurses would have chased Taupe out of her friend's room. But the charge nurse took pity on both of them, especially when Stephanie was admitted with hypothermia and a mild case of frostbite and it became obvious that Taupe was in no hurry to be anywhere else. Taupe saw it as divine intervention, God once again stepping in to put her where He wanted her to be. And it was true: she was simply there in Chicago waiting for something to happen. She had grown up with Stephanie and her big brother, and chances were, big brother would be coming around very soon.

The thought gave her shivers. When Taupe was in high school and even earlier, all the girls would speak in hushed tones around Watson, and how he would become a star tight end. Some even had plans for him to marry them and take them with him when he became successful. But like so many other dreams here in south Chicago, that dream was shattered. In Watson's case, it wasn't a blown knee or a concussion that crushed his football dreams. It was drugs, pure and simple. He didn't take them; he sold them. And when he was arrested, the police record meant that no college would draft him.

Watson became Three-Peat, named for the sad fact that he had been jailed three times for selling drugs. Taupe knew that he was guilty of much more than that, and the same girls who had wished they could be with him in high school now hid in fear of him. At six foot six and two hundred and eighty pounds, Three-Peat was not easily ignored. And he tried to keep his reputation intact.

Three-Peat was also one of the reasons that Taupe was glad to leave South Chicago. She had always known that she would leave the Windy City as soon as she could, but Three-Peat saw her not only as his little sister's girlfriend, but as his property as well. Now, by helping Stephanie out, Taupe was putting her own life at risk.

Taupe decided that the first night was the worst night for Stephanie, and that on the second day, Stephanie would be healed sufficiently that she could call her brother herself and Taupe wouldn't need to be here anymore. At least, that's what she told herself. With that in mind, she got comfortable in the overstuffed chair in Stephanie's room and watched her for a while until she fell asleep.

It was much later that night when Taupe realized that someone else was in the room. Someone very large, looming in the darkness. She took in a gasp of air, then realized that the figure was simply standing over Stephanie, looking at her.

"Sorry," the deep voice said quietly. "I didn't mean to frighten you."

"I was just startled, that's all," Taupe said. "I'm fine."

"How you been, Rosetta?" the voice crooned.

"It's Taupe now," she said. "I never liked Rosetta."

Three-Peat chuckled. "Yeah, another one of those foster home names that gets handed to us without our permission. I hear you're doing good out there in the world."

"Oh, you hear that, do you?" Taupe said. She sat up and stretched in her chair. "Who do you hear that from?"

"I have friends," Three-Peat said. "People who messed up, but decide to do things right, thanks to you and your partners."

"Drug friends?" Taupe said, her voice becoming more accusatory.

"Look, I know you don't approve of what I do and who I am," Three-Peat said. "Reality is, I've changed. I'm trying to help people here on the south side. Things are hard for a lot of people. I'm trying to help the community."

"What? You giving young kids jobs on street corners like in the old days?" Taupe said, an edge in her voice. "You maybe expanding to include thirteen-year-old girls?" Taupe stood up and shook her head. "Watson, you've only and always been about yourself. What makes you think I can believe you've changed?" She shook her head.

"Look, you're here now, so I'm not needed," Taupe said. "I did this for Stephanie, not for you. Look me up when you're really ready to change." She reached for her jacket and turned to go.

"Wait," Three-Peat said, reaching out and grasping her arm. "Don't go."

"Let go of my arm or I'm going to break your hand," Taupe said, speaking through tight lips.

"All right," he said, and loosened his grip. "But just know this. I've been praying. Praying a lot. I've seen how my life has been going, and how Stephanie's life is going. And I do want to change. I believe that God sent you here to help us change. Things are happening here that I think we need your help with." He paused and looked at her, standing in the doorway, facing away from him.

"I know you're a follower of God. Pray about it. If you think this is what God wants you to do, I'll be waiting for you to come back and help us. You know where to find us."

Taupe stood at the doorway for a long moment, the ghosts of her past struggling with the reality of her current mission. She finally sighed audibly and nodded, turning.

"Okay, tell me what's going on and how I can help," she said.

* * *

East Los Angeles

Josh and Pastor Escobar drove up to the abandoned, boarded-up Children of God Mission in the pastor's Lincoln MKZ Hybrid and parked at the curb. Josh noticed that the two teenage boys who were working on the car the last time he was here were still working on it. Last time they were under the hood; this time they had it up on stands and were apparently checking out the driveline.

"Any progress, fellas?" Josh said, as he walked up. The one who was nearest the two men looked at them strangely, then shouted to the house.

"Dad," he said. "Some guys are here to see you."

Pastor Escobar had wisely left his coat jacket in the car and had rolled his shirt sleeves up before they came to the house. Now as the middle-aged man came out, his tattoos matching the ones that Rico Escobar had up and down his arms, they looked like a matched set. Josh expected smiles and grins and handshakes and hugs, but the greeting was strangely serious.

"Herman," Pastor Escobar said to the man approaching. "It's been a long time." He held out his hand to shake, but the other man didn't take it.

"Not long enough," Herman said. *"¿Por qué abandonaste el barrio?"*

"It's complicated," Pastor Escobar said. "I wanted a fresh start."

"What about the rest of us?" Herman said. *"Eras nuestro jefe!"*

Pastor Escobar shook his head. "That was part of the problem. There were too many people looking to me instead of looking to Jesus Christ. I was getting in the way. I felt like I wasn't doing what I was supposed to do."

Josh stepped in. "Gentlemen, we'll all have time to go over this in days to come, but right now we have more important things to do. We need to get the Mission open and running again."

The two boys laughed, and the man shook his head.

"What's so funny?" Josh asked.

Herman shook his head. "They won't let that happen."

"Who? Who won't let that happen?" Pastor Escobar said.

Herman got a sour look on his face and looked down at his two sons, who had crawled out from under the car. At the same time, there was the roaring sound of motorcycles and six bikes and bikers appeared around the corner. They all paused in front of the Mission, then looked at the pastor's Lincoln and laughed. Then they roared off in a cloud of blue smoke.

"Who is that?" Josh asked.

"Those are the Ronin," the boys answered. "The real deal. Not you old has-beens."

* * *

Connie met Adam at the back door of the bookstore that next afternoon. He had made a run to the grocery store and was unloading several forty-pound bags of dog food from the trunk of his car. As he lifted one out, the springs released the car slightly and it raised up, even though three more bags of dog food were still in there. Adam turned and saw Connie walk up and gestured to the other bags.

"Can you grab a bag while you're at it?" Adam said, puffing.

"What, you buy these on sale or something?" Connie asked. "Why so many?"

"If you saw how quickly this hound is going through food, you wouldn't ask that," Adam said. "He must have eaten half a bagful just since this morning."

"You're kidding," Connie said, reaching for a second bag and struggling with the weight. "You've got to be exaggerating. No dog eats that much."

"Maybe," Adam said. "But I'll make you a deal. Either you get that dog housebroken or you're in charge of cleaning up after him. Twenty pounds of dog food makes a lot of dog poop. And I would rather lug dog food than clean up that stuff."

Connie chuckled as they went inside and up the stairs. "I will assume responsibility for his backend leftovers as long as you can provide vittles."

"Deal," Adam said. They entered the apartment and Crash was sitting on the floor with Miracle, trying to teach him a trick.

"This dog is *smart*," Crash said. "Look, I almost got him to stay. Watch." Crash stood up and turned to Miracle who sat watching him, curious. "Stay, Miracle. Stay."

"Has he gotten bigger *overnight?*" Connie said as she came to the top of the stairs and saw the Rottweiler pup.

Miracle stayed where he was, until he saw Connie climb the stairs with her dog food and put it down at the top of the stairs. He suddenly got up and joined her, his stunted tail wagging vigorously.

"Oh look, you ruined it," Crash said. "He was doing fine until you came in here."

"Sorry," Connie said. "It was probably because I brought more dog food."

"I don't think it had anything to do with the food," Adam said. "Look."

Miracle sniffed her hand, then licked it and whined. Adam looked at Crash.

"Looks like Miracle has chosen his master," Adam said.

"So, explain to me how the Heretics work," Crash said. He was brushing Miracle while Connie put the dog food away. Adam had gone downstairs to run the bookstore.

"Well, it all started with Harris Borden," Connie said. "He was called by God to fight this evil corporation called Universal. They worshipped evil angels, three lieutenants of Satan that were planning bad things for the world. Pastor Borden fought them by himself, then he got some help. He went to prison and learned how to survive, how to fight, how to disappear, and how to live on the streets. When he escaped from prison, he recruited some people, mostly street kids, to fight these evil angels with him. People started calling them the Heretics."

"Cool," Crash said. "So, they're kinda like superheroes?"

Connie scrunched her face. "Well, not really. Superheroes aren't real. We're real people. We get hurt. We have problems. We even fight with each other sometimes."

"So, you're a superhero too," Crash said. "Very cool. Do you have special powers?"

"Well, I'm really good at languages," Connie said. "I can speak twelve fluently and I'm learning about eight more."

"Can you fight?"

Connie hesitated, then shook her head. "Taupe has tried to teach me, but I suck at fighting."

"So, you're like the mascot," Crash said. "That's okay, every superhero team needs a mascot."

Connie turned as Crash was talking. Adam had come upstairs and was standing there, expectantly.

"Can you watch the store for a few minutes?" he asked. She nodded. She turned back to Crash.

"Well, I don't mind being the mascot," Connie said. "But you got to remember that the power for these superheroes comes from God, not from themselves."

"What about their nemesis?" Crash asked.

"What?" Connie asked, alarm bells suddenly going off in her head.

"You said Harris Borden fought off three demon lieutenants. Those were the supervillains. Every superhero needs a supervillain. Who is yours?"

Connie stared at Crash, then at Adam. She didn't have an answer, but something told her the enemy would show himself soon enough.

Adam was gone for about an hour, during which time Connie watched the store. Adam had also invested in a collar and leash for Miracle, so Crash decided to take Miracle for a walk. It gave Crash and Miracle a chance to get to know the neighborhood, and Connie a few moments to be alone with her thoughts.

Strange things were going on in Heretics-ville, crazy things that made her uneasy. When she had decided to sign on with the Heretics, she had thought that sure, there would be a learning curve, and that she would have a rough time with some things. But the older, wiser, members would be around to help her understand why things happened the way that they did and how she would eventually fit into it all.

Now the people who could make sense of it all had disappeared, leaving Adam, Connie, and the bookstore behind. On one hand, she felt that was a signal for her to close the shop and go home, bowing to her sister's demand that she be available for her parents in Dallas. It would be so easy to say that was the right thing to do. And yet, despite feeling as if she was swimming up a waterfall, she felt that staying here, sticking with the mission of being a Heretic, and even possibly recruiting some new people, was what God wanted for her. She found herself praying about it constantly, and each time she did, she waited for a feeling that, yes, this is the right thing to do. But there was still that niggling feeling in the back of her mind that she was only fooling herself. That she would never be another Harris Borden, another Taupe, another Josh.

She was still thinking along those lines when Adam returned from his errand. Even though it was still early, she excused herself and decided to walk to her job at The Roadhouse on Sixth Street, hoping it would clear her mind. Even though Bill still hadn't found her a server position, she didn't mind doing stock work in the back, and had even helped him out with his bookkeeping. She suspected that Bill, and the bartender Luther as well, kept her around for conversation more than their need for another worker, but she didn't complain. She enjoyed being around them as well. In addition, when there was a tourist that came in who spoke Mandarin, Japanese or another language that one of the servers didn't know, Connie was happy to help.

She had walked quite a way down Guadalupe, almost to Sixth Street, when she came to Wooldridge Square Park and noticed that several homeless were camping there. One very large man with blonde hair stood up beneath the bough of a cedar tree, over which he had spread a canvas tarp to make a temporary shelter. He was standing facing her, wearing a green surplus army jacket, the setting sun striking him, and she realized that she knew him.

She walked up to him, and the suddenness of her arrival startled the man. He started to go back in his shelter, but after a few seconds Connie's words got his attention.

"Stevie?" she called out. "Sgt. Steven Swanson is that you?" she went up to him and started to hug him but realized that he was uncomfortable with the embrace.

"It's me," Connie said. "Oh, yeah, you probably don't remember me. I helped Josh at the bookstore when you used to come there. Remember Josh? How are you?"

"Josh," Stevie said quietly, as if struggling to remember, then he did. "I was gone for a while. They put me in a prison. They were afraid of me because I like to live out here."

"Yeah, I remember that," Connie said darkly. "But now you're out and free. Can I do anything for you?"

"Where is Josh?" Stevie asked. "I'm awful hungry and Josh was always good about finding me a meal."

Connie shook her head. "Look, Josh isn't around right now. Not sure where he is. But I can get you a meal." She looked at the other homeless who were camped out in the park. "What about your friends here? I suppose they're hungry too."

Stevie nodded. "Your assistance is appreciated."

"Look, I'm on my way to work," Connie said. "When I come back, I promise to bring some food back with me. So don't go away. Okay?"

Connie hurried the several blocks remaining to Sixth Street and The Roadhouse. By the time she got there, she was five minutes late. As Bill opened his mouth to censure her for being late, she interrupted him.

"Look, I know I'm late, Bill, but I have a major request to make," Connie said. "I have a friend. He's a veteran. His name is Staff Sgt. Steven Swanson. He's a marine who has done three tours of duty in Afghanistan and been decorated twice. Now he's suffering from PTSD and is living as a homeless person on the streets here in Austin. Can we feed him tonight?"

Bill stared at Connie, then started laughing. "Sure. Is that all?"

"Well, not really," Connie continued. "It seems like we end up with a lot of leftover food at the end of the night. In fact, this whole street is lined with restaurants that throw away food every night. And all of this is happening while homeless people are going hungry. Do you think we can do something about that?"

Bill laughed again and shook his head. "I love you, Connie, you know that?" He scratched his chin. "Tonight, you round up as much food as you can carry, and you can take it to them. That's from us. Tomorrow, I'll schedule a meeting with the other restaurant owners here on Sixth Street. If you can organize the homeless, as daunting as that may be, I guess I can organize the restaurant owners. Maybe together we can set something up."

"That would be wonderful," Connie said, smiling from ear to ear.

"You're the one who's wonderful," Bill said.

And for the first time that day, Connie felt like she had done something worthwhile.

12

Attacked

What had started as a one-time gesture to feed a friend quickly became a huge enterprise. Connie got another server from the Roadhouse to drive her over later that night with to-go boxes filled with leftover food, which the homeless at the park devoured.

At first, she found they were skeptical about her good intentions, especially when she and her friend Ovid drove up in the Honda hatchback close to midnight and opened the back. However, as soon as the aroma of lasagna, fried chicken and chicken fried steak wafted through the night air, they began to creep out of their makeshift shelters and come forward to investigate. Ovid stayed with the car and the food, while Connie quickly went over to find Stevie. She expected to find him asleep in his lean-to but found him helping a mother and two children get settled for the night. He was surprised when Connie appeared.

"Dinner is on," Connie said brightly. "Anyone hungry?"

Stevie raised his wrist and looked at his watch. "It's kind of late." While he spoke, the mother and small boy and girl leaped up and disappeared in the direction of the food.

"Yeah, sorry about that," Connie said. "Listen, we can do this on a regular basis. I worked out a plan with the restaurant owners. But I'll need your help. You interested?"

Stevie frowned. "Are you sure you want me? I mean, I'm not an organizer. I just like to be left alone."

Connie gestured at what he was doing. "Look at you. You're helping this family out without even thinking. This'll give you a chance to help even more people. But I can't do it alone. I need you, Stevie. Sgt. Swanson."

Stevie stared at her for a long moment, and she saw him transform in front of her eyes.

"Let me know what you need me to do," he said quietly, firmly.

It was well after midnight before Connie made it to the dorm room and her own bed. It took less than ten minutes for her to shower, brush her teeth, put on her nightclothes, and fall asleep.

That night, she dreamed of Marita again.

The dream wasn't specific in details. It was more a feeling than it was factual. But when she woke up, she once again felt that she was being led to help her friend. How she would help her, she didn't know. All that she knew was that God—she was pretty sure it was God—was calling her to do something. And after all she had been through, she wasn't going to turn God down.

Marita no longer took the Calligraphy class that Connie had signed up for. In fact, after that first day, Marita had dropped it. Sadly, Connie felt like she was the reason her friend was no longer in the class. But why would someone drop a class, just because someone else was in it? Wasn't that juvenile behavior? Or was that some other sort of signal?

Connie didn't see Marita on the large campus anywhere else, other than on rare occasion in the hallway. So how was she going to locate her? She knew that she was living in the home of a former professor who was active with the Mystics, the group of Wiccans that the two of them had escaped from almost a year before. It was one of the biggest mistakes in Connie's life, thinking that she wanted to be a witch. And it almost proved to be fatal. But even after they were kidnapped by the Mystics, held in a dungeon, then rescued, Marita decided to return to the Mystics on her own accord.

Should she try to find out where they were located these days? She didn't even know the name of this former professor. If she did, would it be wise to go over and knock on their door and ask to speak to Marita? Is that what Harris Borden would do?

Connie mulled over the idea, then decided to take the chicken's way out. She decided to visit the records office and see if she could get

Marita's class schedule. Then she could wait and ambush Marita as she came out of class, hopefully catching her alone so they could talk.

She was thinking about all these things during Calligraphy class while Prof. Brinkmeyer continued in her lecture about cuneiform. Finally, class was over, and the students started filing out. Connie started following them, mindlessly, thinking that she needed to go to the Records office.

No, a voice told her. *Go to the cafeteria.*

I'm not even hungry, she told herself, then hesitated. If God is trying to tell her something, maybe give her a hint about how to solve her problem, why wasn't she listening?

"Cafeteria it is," Connie muttered to herself, then wondered if it was still open at ten in the morning. She followed the line of students through the Commons and to the cafeteria. It was mostly empty, with just a couple of people sitting around the edges. And toward the back, sitting by herself, Connie saw Marita.

She was just finishing some scrambled eggs and orange juice but didn't seem to be in any hurry. Connie noticed the way that Marita was dressed, and it rang a bell. It was the outfit that she liked to wear when they went out together after work. Connie had always told her that it made her look happy. But right now, Marita looked anything but happy.

"I guess they don't provide breakfast at the faculty home where you're living these days," Connie quipped as she approached. Immediately, she regretted the words.

"Prof. Hughes is out of town for a week," Marita said, looking up frostily. "I was just leaving." She started to get up, but Connie held out her hand, palm down, and Marita hesitated.

"Please, Marita, sit for a minute, will you?" Connie said. Marita settled back in her chair and Connie sat down in the chair opposite her. Marita looked very uncomfortable.

"Look, Marita, I know we've grown apart," Connie said. "But I still care about you very much. I see you suffering. I see it in your eyes. Please, is there anything I can do to help you?"

112

Marita opened her mouth to speak but said nothing. She looked over Connie's shoulder as if someone were there, then looked down.

"Things are very complicated for me," Marita said. "I know you mean well, Connie, but you would only get hurt if you tried to help."

Connie looked down and saw that Marita was gripping the edge of her food tray tightly.

"I have friends," Connie said. "You would be amazed at what we can do."

Marita stared at Connie, and Connie could see that she was on the edge of tears.

"Just stay out of it, Connie," she said. "For your own sake, stay away from me."

"I can't do that, Marita," Connie said.

"Stay *away* from me," Marita suddenly shouted, throwing her tray away from her, the food flying everywhere. "You can't help me." She leaped to her feet and marched out the exit of the cafeteria. Connie watched her go. And then Connie noticed a man who had been sitting behind her, against the wall. He stood and followed Marita out the door.

* * *

"And then she threw her food tray across the cafeteria, right before she marched out of the room." Connie was explaining what happened to Adam at the bookstore, while Crash and Miracle were once again out on a walk.

"And that was it?" Adam said. He stood on a ladder, putting books on a high shelf while she talked.

"Yeah, pretty much, except this creepy guy was sitting by the wall right behind where I was sitting. I remember she kept looking over my shoulder at him as she talked, as if he were listening to our conversation."

"And she said that things were complicated, and that you would only get hurt if you got involved," Adam said. "Huh." He looked at the

113

book in his hands. "Do you know why we have three copies of James Joyce's *Ulysses*? Especially since we haven't sold a copy in, like, ever?"

"No telling," Connie said. "I think it was Josh's favorite book." She frowned. "She said that the retired professor she lived with was named Hughes. Do you know a Prof. Hughes?"

"I don't, but we have some old university annuals around here," Adam said. "He's bound to be in one of them. Get a first name and then Google him."

"Here they are," Connie said, walking down a long aisle. "Does anyone ever buy this stuff?"

"Not that I know of," Adam said. "Look back about five, then ten years."

"How are you doing on breaking that encryption on that hard drive?" Connie said as she kept looking down the aisle.

"Still working on it," Josh said. "Like most puzzles, easy if you know the answer. Hard if you don't."

Connie pulled the annuals out and began searching. A few minutes later, she came across a name. She put her finger on it.

"Dr. Latham Hughes, professor of English," she said. "Specializing in Shakespeare. Retired seven years ago. Listen to what he wrote under his name: 'Hell is empty, and all the devils are here.' -W. Shakespeare."

She snapped the annual shut and looked at Adam.

"Cheery guy," Adam said.

"I don't like it, but it looks like I need to infiltrate that place," Connie said, her mouth in a thin line.

"Infiltrate what place?" Crash said, as he and Miracle came bounding into the room. Miracle made a beeline for Connie, and almost knocked her over. She put hands on either side of the big puppy's head and gave him a big smooch atop his head.

"Oh, what a good dog you are!" Connie said, rubbing him vigorously. "You're so sweet!"

"Infiltrate what place?" Crash repeated. "I'm in."

"You can't infiltrate that place," Adam said. "They know your face. Not only were you all over the news, if there are any people left over from the old Mystics, they'll know you right away."

"Well, you can't do it," Connie said.

"Why not," Adam said.

"What if your father is involved? What if your aunt is involved?"

"My father is in Europe somewhere and my aunt is in prison," Adam said.

"Guys," Crash said. "What about me?"

"No," both Adam and Connie said simultaneously. "You're a kid," Connie added.

"What do we do then?" Connie said. "Do we try to get hold of Harris? Or Josh?"

"I still think I'm the best candidate," Adam said.

"Let me think about it," Connie said. "Let me pray about it."

* * *

"Aren't you supposed to be at work in an hour?" Adam asked Connie, as she continued to play with Miracle and Crash in the back of the bookstore.

"Yeah, so?" Connie said. "You offering to take me there?"

"Can't. You know our doors are open 'til seven. Later if we get actual paying customers. But it might help business if you and Crash took your four-legged wrecking machine and left for a little while. I know he's adorable, but some people find a dog in a bookstore a bit distracting."

Connie chuckled and tugged on Miracle's leash.

"C'mon Crash," she said. "Let's take Miracle down the street and see if there is any trouble we can chase away from the neighborhood."

"Miracle is good for that!" Crash said as they headed for the door. "Someday I am going to teach him to do parkour with me."

"I'd pay good money to see that," Adam shouted after them, his head down and still looking at the list of books he was trying to organize. The door closed, and suddenly Adam found the room blissfully quiet. Organizing books called for him to make decisions that he felt uncomfortable making, decisions that Josh would ordinarily make. He wondered to himself how long Josh would be gone and whether he should start making those decisions on his own. One of them was obvious: money. The rent was due in a few days, and as an employee, he hadn't been paid in several weeks. He didn't have legal access to the bookstore's bank account to make any transactions. The more he thought about it, the more convinced he was that he *had* to hack that hard drive and find out what he could about where he was.

He's been working on it for several nights, and come close, but was missing the algorithm key. And as he continued organizing books, the key suddenly came to him. *Of course*, he thought.

He looked around at the empty bookstore, then at the clock. Five forty-five. An hour and fifteen minutes left to go. An hour of looking at an empty bookstore while their future waited upstairs. *No one is coming*, he told himself. He nodded to himself, then trotted to the front door and put up the closed sign and locked the door. Then he turned and bounded up the stairs.

He sat down at Josh's desk and pulled open his laptop. The screen shone open, asking for the key. Adam paused and then typed: ULYSSES.

The screen cleared and several file folders revealed themselves to him.

"At last," Adam said. He immediately pulled out a flash drive and began doing a global copy. As he did so, a message came up: "Copying complete in 35 minutes."

Then Adam bounded down the stairs to reopen the store. When he got halfway down the stairs, he discovered he wasn't alone. Three burly men in heavy coats and black ski masks were standing in the middle of the store aisle, looking at him. One of them held a police baton, a second held a baseball bat.

"Well, hello," the one in the front said. He stepped toward Adam.

Adam chuckled. "If you've come for a robbery, boy, you're picked the wrong place." Adam took another step down the stairs and stopped. "Can I offer you guys some coffee? We don't have much in the cash register, but we have great coffee."

"Are you Josh Brown?" the front man said. Adam shook his head.

"You're the second man who asked me that this week," he said. "No, I just work here. My name is Adam."

The man in the front sighed. "Well, Adam, you're going to tell us where Josh Brown is, or else we are going to tear this place apart. And you with it."

Adam looked around. "Be my guest. As you can see, it's just books. Nothing more than that."

The big man in front chuckled and looked at his friends. "That's not what we were told. You know something that we need to learn. We'll start with the whereabouts of Josh Brown and go from there." He reached into his pocket and started to pull out something that looked like a gun. Adam didn't wait to see what it was but turned and ran up the stairs. He heard smashing behind him and visualized the two men with bats and batons working over the cash register and the bookshelves. *That's fine*, he thought. *We can fix all that a lot easier than we can fix me.*

He grabbed the door handle just as a big hand closed around his ankle and started to pull. The pull of the big man made Adam lose his balance, and he collapsed on the stairs. The man began to pull Adam toward him. Adam rolled over onto his back and kicked the man full in the face with his Vans shoe.

The man grunted and jerked back, letting go of Adam and staggering backward on the stairs. He grabbed the railing and started to fall back to the floor but caught himself. In the meantime, Adam turned and clambered on hands and feet the last few steps up the stairs into Josh's apartment. He slammed the door after him and turned the deadbolt.

*That will hold them just about….*he thought, and then the door was slammed by the men on the other side. It was a thin interior door, and

Adam didn't have hope that it would hold for long. But in the meantime, he looked at Josh's computer and saw that the download was still in progress.

Thirty-nine minutes to completion.

"Dang," Adam said. He pulled out the flash drive and pocketed it, then did a hard shut down of the computer. A second later, the door flew off the hinges.

On the other side stood the three men who had been there downstairs.

"Fool," the man in front said. "Where did you think you could run?"

"Look," one of the others said. "There's Brown's laptop. That's all we need. Let's get it and go." He reached over and pulled it free from its power cord.

"Wait," the man in front said. "One more thing left to do."

He stepped forward and slammed Adam in the jaw with an uppercut. Adam flew back onto the floor and saw stars, the pain shooting through his head. He looked up at the legs of the three men.

"Now we can leave," he said. Adam watched as the three men disappeared down the stairs. 𝒱

13

Self Defense

It didn't take Connie and Crash long to realize something was wrong when they got back from their walk with Miracle. The sign on the front door said, "Closed," but the door stood open, with the deadbolt broken. Books lay strewn all over the floor, and as Connie looked, she could see the coffeemaker broken and scattered on the floor on the back side of the front desk.

"Where's Adam?" she hissed at Crash. "Adam? Adam!" she shouted. Crash let go of Miracle, and the dog made an immediate run upstairs, pushing the door open. A moment later, Adam appeared at the door, holding his head. Connie gasped when she saw his bruised jaw.

"What happened!" she gasped. She ran across the floor and up the stairs to meet Adam, who was stumbling down awkwardly. Miracle was both excited to see Adam and concerned, and in his own playful way was trying to help, which meant he was no help at all. He jumped in front of Adam as he tried to step down the stairs, and Adam finally had to push the dog out of the way. Adam and Connie then came down the stairs and sat on a couch at the base of the stairs.

"Are you all right?" Connie asked, and Adam nodded, then winced.

"Three guys…big dudes," Adam said. "They were looking for Josh."

"Well, he wasn't here," Connie said. "So, what did they get?"

"His computer," Adam said.

"His computer!" Connie echoed. "But that's terrible. We've got to get it back."

"They didn't get everything," Adam said. "Remember it's passworded and the hard drive is encrypted. I was able to finally break the encryption, but I couldn't download it in time. But they shouldn't be able to access it; at least it will take them some time. So we are still at square one as far as paying bills and contacting other Heretics."

Connie sighed. "Well, break in or not, I still have to get to work. I'll see you guys later."

Adam shook his head. "Let me drive you. It doesn't look like we're in any position to be open tonight anyway. And I need the company."

The next morning, the usual Philosophy class was cancelled and the three presenters for the "Science, Magic, or Faith" workshop were scheduled to meet with Prof. Valencia. Connie was both excited and nervous. She knew that the other presenters weren't in her class and she probably didn't know them, so this would be her first opportunity to meet them.

Prof. Valencia introduced them to Connie as Patrick Jackson, a senior double majoring in physics and philosophy, and Katie Dawkins, a junior philosophy major. Patrick wore a perpetual smug, arrogant look on his face, and Connie wondered if she had ever seen him in the hallway. On the other hand, she worried that Katie was one of the girls she had run into when she was involved with the Mystics.

"We have three weeks until the conference," Prof. Valencia told the three of them. "I want you all to understand the ground rules and the purpose of this conference. This isn't a debate, although it may come across that way to some people. The purpose of this event is for people to see that there are other people who think differently than they do, and that their way of thinking may not be the only perspective possible."

Patrick raised his hand.

"Yes, Patrick?" Prof. Valencia said.

"Does that mean I have to believe in faith and magic the way I do in science?" he asked. "Because I'm telling you right now, I don't."

"No, you don't have to," Prof. Valencia said. "But I won't have personal insults leveled at other presenters, or smug remarks intended to demean those who believe differently than you do."

"Yeah, Patrick," Katie said. "No making fun of someone who believes in magic."

"It's not real, you know," Patrick said.

"We'll see," Katie said. "Let me show you a thing or two."

"All right," Prof. Valencia said, holding his hands out to quiet them both. "Now we will begin with a brief introduction by each of you, followed by three questions from the moderator, which is me. You'll each get the same question."

"Will we know what the questions are beforehand?" Connie asked.

"No," Prof. Valencia said. "This will be strictly spontaneous responses. Then we will open it up to questions from the audience. This is where it might get a little...shall I say...lively? We have done similar events like this in the past, and there's no telling what kind of questions or comments will come from the audience. But we'll try to keep them courteous."

Prof. Valencia looked at the three of them. "All right? Now I have someone I want you three to meet. He's our sponsor for this event this year. And he's a big supporter of this school. I've only met him in the past day or so. But I know you'll like him." He gestured to someone standing outside the doorway and the door opened. In stepped a slight man in a suit.

"Hello," the man said quietly.

"I'd like to introduce the three of you to Dr. Anais Singleton."

As Connie looked at the formally dressed man, who approached them innocently enough, she couldn't help but notice that the hairs started to rise on the backs of her arms.

Anais Singleton didn't have much to say that morning, and he sat watching and listening as Connie and the others went through the preliminaries in preparation for the conference. But Connie never felt comfortable with the middle-aged man, and she didn't know why. He was polite and kind to everyone he talked to and nodded politely when she said goodbye at the end.

Still, she thought about him all the way back to the bookstore where she decided she would check on Adam and the condition of the store. She found the "Closed" sign still up and Adam working with Crash to put up books. He seemed to brighten when Connie arrived.

"We're going to need a new cash register," Adam told her. "They bashed it pretty good."

Connie shrugged. "If I recall, Josh got that one second-hand down the street at Edwardo Sepulveda's antique store. I can check with him and see if he has another one."

Adam turned his head, then winced again. "I've got to stop doing that."

"You probably need to have that looked at," Connie said, stepping forward and looking at his bruised jaw where the fist had hit him. "You might have a concussion."

"I don't have a concussion," Adam said. "What I have is a sore head, a broken bookstore and a need to get stuff done."

"Well, at least take a break," Connie said, grasping his arm and leading him over to the couch where they had sat the night before. "You know, break? You can afford that, can't you?"

"Sure. You look like you want to talk. What's your mind?"

"We had our first planning session for the philosophy conference coming up," Connie said. "Prof. Valencia introduced me to the other two presenters."

"Oh, the mad scientist and the witch," Crash said from across the room. "Did he have hair sticking out? Did she have a pointy hat?"

Adam chuckled and Connie shook her head.

"No, but it's going to be a challenge anyway," Connie said. "I think the science guy is going to be tough. He's a physics/philosophy double major and I don't think he likes Christians."

"Well, I have faith in you," Adam said. "We'll be in the back row praying for you."

"In the back row? I expect you to be in the front row!"

Adam and Crash laughed.

"Anyway, that's not what really concerned me," Connie said. "Prof. Valencia introduced us to the conference's sponsor while we were there. This creepy guy named Anais Singleton."

Adam frowned, then said, "Hmm."

"What?"

"I could be wrong, but I think he's the same guy who came by the bookstore looking for Josh and information about the Heretics the night that you guys arrived with Miracle."

Connie stared at Adam, then shook her head in amazement.

"Wait. Some stranger comes by here late at night asking about the Heretics and you don't think to say anything to me about it?"

"Well, he seemed like a nice guy."

Connie's mouth dropped open.

"I cannot believe what I'm hearing, Adam," she said. "Don't you think I would like to know these things?"

Adam shrugged. "Okay, I messed up. I should have told you. But the guy seemed harmless. I told him what I knew, which was pretty much nothing, and he was on his way."

Connie frowned. "Well, I don't like it. Him seeing both of us like that. Let's put him on our suspicious list from this point on."

Adam gave her a two-fingered salute. "Aye, captain."

"What can I do?" Connie turned to see Crash watching them.

"Stay out of trouble," Adam responded.

"Wait," Connie said. "There's something that Crash can actually do here."

"Really?" Crash's eyes lit up.

Connie nodded. "You know how to get around the city without using the streets. You also have connections with a lot of people. It's time we start watching what's going on. This Mr. Singleton and this break-in are too coincidental. Someone knows something, I'm sure." She looked at Crash. "Talk to people. Talk to your fellow parkour buddies. Talk to the cops. See what you can find out."

She reached out and patted Crash on the shoulder.

"You now have two important responsibilities around here, Crash," she said. "Surveillance and dog walker."

"Cool," Crash said. "I won't fail you."

"Just don't get hurt," Connie said. "I'll kill you if you do."

Crash grinned back at her.

Connie left early for work that evening because she wanted to check with Stevie on the plans for coordinating food distribution for the homeless. She stopped by the park where she had seen him a few nights before, and there was Roberta, the mother with three children who Stevie had been helping that night. She was working on a notepad, writing down names.

"Stevie is over by the Interstate organizing the giveaway there," she said. "He put me in charge of distribution at this location." The young mother shook her head. "Heaven knows how he talked me into taking that much responsibility, but he has a knack for organization. You were right to choose him to help with this project." She paused and looked at Connie seriously. "You and he are helping a lot of people."

Connie smiled back at her. "Thank you for your help as well," she said. "If you hadn't agreed to help, he probably wouldn't have been able to help those people in other locations. I'm just blessed to be part of all of this."

Connie hugged Roberta and left the park, headed toward Sixth Street, knowing that she wouldn't get a chance to see Stevie before she got to work. She continued down Guadalupe Street and cut across to Sixth Street. But when she turned a corner into a connecting alley, she was faced by the shadow of a large man in front of her, holding what looked like a pipe or long stick. She stopped, unsure. A moment later, Stevie stepped out of the shadows using a measured pace she had never seen him use.

"Stevie!" Connie said, catching her breath. "You scared me there for a moment. I thought you were over by I-35."

"I heard there was an attack at the bookstore last night," Stevie said, his voice strangely smooth and deep. "I was concerned about you."

Connie saw that Stevie held a long wooden pole in his hand. "Yeah, they broke in and took Josh's computer and hit Adam. But he's okay." She hesitated. "What's that you have in your hands there?"

"It's called a bo staff," Stevie said. "I thought it was time you learned how to defend yourself."

Connie laughed. "Yeah, well, Taupe tried to teach me self-defense and we both agreed that it was a lost cause. I may have a talent for languages, but I'm worthless when it comes to putting one foot in front of the other."

"Nonsense," Stevie said. "Come here. I want to show you something."

"Stevie, I don't have time…."

"Come here."

Connie realized that Stevie was more serious than at any time she had ever seen him. She bit her lip and took two steps forward and met Stevie in the middle of the alley.

"Take the staff," he said.

She took it from him. It was about five feet long and surprisingly heavy.

"Feel the weight of it. Feel the balance. Move it from your left hand to your right. Like this." He took it back and twirled it around his hand. Then he handed it back to her. "Now you."

She tried to do the same thing but dropped the stick.

"See, I'm a klutz," she began, but he stopped her.

"Listen to me," he said. "You can't just dismiss this. You can't say, 'I can't do this, so oh well.' If you don't learn how to defend yourself, others will hurt you. Maybe kill you. And it's going to happen very soon. So listen to me." He took the staff and pointed it at her, tapping several places on her body.

"Knees. Groin. Stomach. Head. Hit any one of these and you can incapacitate the other person. If you are being chased, go for the knees or the groin. If you are serious and want to stop them permanently, go for the head."

Connie opened her mouth to respond but couldn't find the words. Stevie thrust the bo staff into her hands.

"Keep it with you," he said. "It could save your life."

Connie had known that becoming a Heretic was serious business, that there was a risk of being hurt or killed, but now she was drawing other people into her commitment. And she thought more and more about that while she was at work at the Roundhouse, and even when she headed home that night. The one consolation was that even as she walked home in the late hours that night, she didn't feel quite so vulnerable as she carried the five-foot bo staff with her. It was heavy, was carved with intricate designs and seemed to be made of very hard wood. She hadn't had an opportunity to examine it very closely when she was at work, or while she was walking, so she was determined that she would look at it when she got to the dorm.

The next morning was Friday. She had her Calligraphy class in the morning and then she was free. She raced over to the bookstore to share her new bo staff with Adam and Crash. When she got there, Adam had just opened the bookstore for business and was sweeping up.

"Where's Crash?" she asked. "I have something I think he'll like."

"He left a note over there," Adam said, not looking up. He was neither happy nor sad, and Connie wondered why. She wandered over to the main desk and looked at the yellow pad where Crash had scrawled the note:

Guys:

I now im not yet pulin my wait. But I want to. So I plan to help by invistigaten the grup you call the Mistics. I plan on askin if I can join them today. Don try to stop me. I now wat im doing. —Crash

"First thing when he gets back, we need to teach him how to spell," Adam said, still not looking up.

Connie stared at the paper for a long time, not believing what she was reading. Then she turned to Adam.

"This is not the time to joke, Adam," Connie said. "He's just a kid."

"I know he's just a kid," Adam replied. "But what do you expect me to do? He was gone before I got up this morning."

"Well, maybe if you took a little more responsibility, he wouldn't have run off like this."

Adam threw down his broom. "Blast it! You act like we're married and he's our son! He's not ours! He's an independent human being that you just happened to find out on the street. You need to let him live his life. He wants to help? So let him."

Connie shook her head. "You're an idiot."

The chime at the top of the door rang and they both realized that someone had entered. They both turned, wondering if it was Crash. Instead, they saw that it was a young man.

"I have a message here for Constance Simescu," he said. He held up an envelope.

"I'm Constance," Connie said. He gave her the envelope and left.

Despite what had happened a moment before, Adam came over and looked as she opened the small envelope up. Inside was a card. It read:

"Connie: I know you can speak French and Italian. You have 24 hours to learn Hungarian as well. I will send you an e-ticket. Be prepared to leave in five hours." --Harris. **𝖛**

14

Weekend in Budapest

Now you have a chance to prove yourself, Connie thought several times over the next few hours. *Don't blow it.*

She'd never told Harris Borden that she was fluent in both French and Italian, which she was, of course. But then it made sense that he would know that about her. Chances are, he knew a lot of things about a lot of people, especially those who were or wanted to be Heretics. It wasn't usual that a boss could call his employee and say, "Hey, here's 24 hours. Learn a foreign language." Most people would say, "Are you out of your freaking mind?"

But Harris knew Connie, possibly better than Connie knew Connie. She took pride in the fact that she already knew twelve languages, and in her spare time was learning eight more. But it was her spare time. She'd never really taken it seriously. Maybe it was too easy, a hobby, and that's why she had dropped out of the linguistics program. She could have ended up with a graduate degree and teaching somewhere like her sister; maybe even gotten rich and famous. Who knows? But deep down, Connie knew that she didn't want to use her talent that way. She wanted to use it for God. And now Harris was giving her that chance.

But twenty-four hours? The pressure was on. Of course, Connie knew what to do. The first thing she did was bow her head in prayer. She knew her abilities, but this…this was humbling.

"God," she prayed. "I need a miracle. You have blessed me. You have blessed the Heretics and Harris Borden up to this point. But Harris needs me to do this thing that seems impossible, and I don't want to let him down. Help me not to let him down."

Then she logged on and purchased three different language apps for her phone, buying everything having to do with Hungarian from them. Then she bought two recent bestsellers as Hungarian audiobooks as well. That would take care of the hearing and understanding part of the language, but she would need opportunities to practice it in the next day as well. So she found a Hungarian dating website that she joined. That would come later.

That was in the first hour. She packed her bag, including an ample quantity of granola bars, and her passport, which she was finally going to get a chance to use. After that, she checked her email and saw that indeed, Harris had sent her an e-ticket to Budapest from Austin with connecting flights in Dallas and Frankfurt. She wouldn't get any sleep, that was for sure. But it was bound to be an adventure.

Adam, the true friend that he was, drove her to the airport when it was time. On the way, they talked about Crash, her trip and what to do about the strange man named Anais Singleton.

"Look," Adam said. "He hasn't done anything dangerous. He didn't attack either you or me. He hasn't made any threats. I don't know what the big deal it."

"Adam, you have to admit that there are bad people out there who never hold a gun or raise a fist. Your dad is a good example of that." Connie scrunched her face as she said it. "Sorry."

"No problem," Adam said. "Yeah, but Dad did make threats. I heard some of those threats. This guy was polite, and just asked questions. I probably would have given him anything he wanted."

"That in itself is suspicious, don't you think?" Connie said. "Look, let me talk to Harris about him. We'll see what he thinks. In the meantime, just be careful. And watch for Crash. I really don't know what to do about that situation."

"Yeah," Adam said. "We say anything to the police, and Crash will end up in a foster home. As good as that may be for him, I don't think he wants that. And frankly, I don't think we want that either."

"I understand now how my parents felt when I snuck out after curfew," Connie said. "Sometimes all you can do for the kiddos is pray." She looked at Adam. "So, let's pray. A lot."

"Gotcha, captain," Adam said.

Thankfully, Harris had booked Connie in first class for the entire trip, with Wi-Fi available throughout the journey. It was a one-hour flight to Dallas, followed by an hour layover there, then a nine-hour flight to Frankfurt with another two-hour layover. Six bleary hours after that, Connie's plane would be landing in Budapest International Airport. But the nineteen hours that Connie spent in transit wasn't lost reading magazines, in conversation or even in sleep. Thanks to having internet, Connie was able to immerse herself in the Hungarian language the entire time. From the time Adam dropped her off in Austin until she went through customs in Frankfurt, she was continually listening to and interacting with Babbel, Rosetta Stone and DuoLingo. She ignored any calls for conversation, only asked for water from the flight attendant when they came by and made three restroom breaks.

After she left Frankfurt, she switched gears and logged onto AmourHungaria, the Russian-based dating app that she had read was popular for Hungarian singles. She quickly built her profile, stressing that she was only interested in talking to other singles who would speak Hungarian.

"*Örülök, hogy megismerhetem,*" Connie said to Oleg, the first young man who logged on to chat with her.

"Hello, sweetheart," he answered back in English. "Why so formal? Let's get to know each other."

"*Meg akarok tanulni magyarul,*" she said. "I want to learn Hungarian. If you can't speak it, then this conversation is over."

"Okay, okay," Oleg said. "Why are you interested in learning Hungarian?" he rattled off in the language.

Connie smiled back and relaxed. She continued in Hungarian. "*Köszönöm.* I appreciate it. I'm on my way to Budapest on a business trip and want to be able to converse with others when I get there."

Oleg smiled back at her slyly. "You know, Budapest is a very western city. Most people there speak English as well. Or at least Russian. *A ty govorish' po russki?*"

"Yes, I speak Russian too," Connie said back in Hungarian, annoyed that he was getting off the subject. "Look, if you can't speak Hungarian, I will find someone who will."

Oleg looked hurt. "I thought we made a connection," he said in Hungarian. "Look, while you are in Budapest, if you want to hook up, call me, why don't you? I can show you around."

"I appreciate your generosity, but I don't think I'll be in town that long," Connie said. "Thanks for the chat, Oleg." She disconnected from him and tried another dating partner.

Three frustrating conversations later, most of them in English, she realized not only that most of the people her age in Budapest were fluent in English, but that they were more eager to speak English to an American than she was to speak Hungarian. She switched over to listen to an audiobook in Hungarian. It ended up being a smarmy romance novel, and that frustrated her more than before.

Realizing that she was coming closer to Budapest and would be landing in a little over an hour, she muttered to herself.

"*Ez reménytelen*," she groaned. "*Feladom*. I give up." She leaned back in her seat and sighed.

"Don't give up," the elderly woman in the next seat said to her in Hungarian. "You are coming to the land of eternal hope." Connie looked up at the woman, dressed in dark, plain clothes, who up to this point had remained silent and engrossed in a book. Now she turned and smiled at Connie. "I'm sorry. I couldn't help but overhear your attempts at conversation. If you want to learn to speak a language, don't you think it would be better to speak with someone face to face?"

Connie looked back at the woman, who twinkled back at her with a mischievous grin. Connie grinned back.

"Absolutely. *Teljesen*," she said. Connie held out her hand. "I'm Connie. And thank you."

The woman identified herself as Sara Lutz and was living in Stockholm but was originally from a small village outside of Budapest. Sara's sister had died recently, and she was coming to help take care of her sister's family until they could sort things out. They talked about

Connie's family, and Sara was intrigued to know that Connie's parents were from Romania but had fled to America during the Communist rule. She was also fascinated by the fact that Connie lived in Texas.

"I thought everyone wore cowboy boots and tall hats there," Sara said, grinning.

Connie grinned back. "Not quite. Although a few of my friends do."

They talked incessantly during the rest of the trip into Budapest, and to Connie's surprise, Connie forgot that she was trying to learn a new language but instead just focused on getting to know more about Sara. Finally, it was time to deplane. Connie reached over and hugged Sara.

"Thank you," she said. "*Köszönöm.* You have given me much more than a chance to learn Hungarian."

"*Isten veled,*" Sara whispered in her ear. "Go with God."

They left the plane and quickly went through immigration and customs. Connie watched as the guard vigorously stamped her passport and handed it back to her.

"Enjoy your stay," the officer said. Connie nodded and smiled in return.

On the other side of the glass door, Harris Borden stood waiting. He took her bag and turned to walk quickly to the curb.

"Hello, Harris," Connie said, looking at him. "Aren't you going to say hi, or even ask me if I learned Hungarian like you asked me to?" She looked at him and saw his face more serious than she had ever seen it.

"Later," he barked. "Right now, we need to get to the hotel. We have four teams waiting for us." He pushed through the crowds in the terminal and Connie hurried to keep up with him.

"So, is this all going to be business, or will I get a chance to do some sightseeing while I'm here?" Connie asked casually. "Cuz I've never been to Europe, much less Budapest."

Harris turned in the middle of the crowd and grasped her arms tightly.

"Listen to me," he hissed. "I know I'm asking a lot of you, but I had no choice. We have four teams that were part of the original plan to train new Heretics. One of them is responsible for killing those innocent volunteers. If they find out what we're trying to do, chances are they'll do the same thing to us." He stared at her, looking for some sort of recognition.

"So, I guess that's a no on the sightseeing," Connie said slowly.

Harris shook his head in frustration, then charged ahead and Connie followed him through the crowd. A few moments later, they were at the line of cabs outside the terminal.

"Ritz-Carlton Hotel," he said to the cab driver, as he and Connie climbed in the back of the cab with her small bag.

"*Melyik irány ez?*" Serge, the cab driver barked back at him.

"Great," Harris said, frowning. "We have the only cab driver here who doesn't speak English."

"He's asking where the hotel is, which direction," Connie said.

"It's over by the university," Harris said. "On the Pest side of the river."

"*Pesten van, a folyo mellett,*" Connie told Serge, and he nodded and turned to drive out into traffic.

Connie sat back and looked at Serge, then at Harris. She saw a slight grin come across each of their faces.

"Wait," she said. "You did that on purpose. That was a test!"

Harris and the cab driver began to laugh. Connie shook her head.

"One that you passed with flying colors," Harris said. "Congratulations."

"Hungarian is a hard language to master," Serge said in heavily accented English. "I am impressed."

Connie frowned, then shook her head and grinned.

"Sorry I was tough on you back there in the terminal," Harris said. "But you understand why."

Connie nodded. "I understand. And I won't let you down." She hesitated. "Harris, can I ask you something?"

"Of course," Harris looked out the window at the passing traffic as they left the airport and headed for the hotel.

"The people we're dealing with are educated. Most of them speak English fluently. In fact, even if you have me translate your words into Hungarian, chances are they will respond back in English. Why did you need me here? Why the rush to learn Hungarian? Why all the secrecy?"

Harris smiled a painful little smile.

"Years ago, I used to believe that if a person called himself a Christian, you could believe that what he said was true," Harris said it and sighed. "Now I know better. The world is a complicated place. Someone is responsible for telling our enemies what our plans were. Someone is responsible for ten people being killed on their way to join our ranks. They aren't likely to admit to our faces that they did it, but if there is more than one of them, this meeting will give them a chance to reveal themselves. And we'll find out who they are, once and for all."

Connie stared at Harris, thinking.

"And if you find out who betrayed us?" she asked. "What will you do then?"

Harris didn't answer for a long moment, then shrugged.

"That's something I need to pray about."

Serge unloaded Connie's small bag from the cab outside the Ritz-Carlton Hotel, the upscale hotel a few blocks from the Danube River, with a mixture of government buildings, modern hotels and what looked like ancient castles surrounding them. Connie's mouth dropped open as she tried to take in the sights around her. She caught at least six different languages being spoken within earshot and was pleased to realize that she understood five of them.

"Close your mouth," Harris said gruffly. "You look like a tourist."

"I *am* a tourist," Connie barked back. "This is fantastic."

"Wait 'til you see our suite upstairs," Harris said. "The Foundation is paying for it."

Connie followed Harris to the elevator where he inserted a key and then punched the button marked PH. *Penthouse*, Connie thought, and a thrill went through her. A moment later, the doors opened directly into a massive hotel suite.

"Normally the curtains would be pulled open, but Bobby is working in the other room," Harris said. "He wanted it dark."

"Bobby is here?" Connie echoed.

"In the flesh," Bobby said, wheeling into the entryway in his wheelchair, a big grin on his face. "Hello, Connie." Connie stepped forward and hugged him. "Don't worry, boss. You haven't missed anything. The British team just got here a couple of minutes before you."

"Okay, then let me explain how this works," Harris said to Connie, loud enough for Bobby to hear. "I'm going into a top-secret conference with four teams from Great Britain, France, Italy and Hungary to discuss what happened. Two of their representatives will be at the meeting, but the rest of their team will be in their suites, except for the locals. Yesterday I put cameras in the suites of the different teams to determine if they will say anything incriminating while they're here."

"So you want me to listen in on their conversations in the rooms," Connie said. "Isn't that a stretch? What if they're just careful and don't say anything?"

Harris looked at Bobby, who shrugged. "Then we just bought you a free weekend in Budapest for nothing."

The hotel phone buzzed in the corner, and Harris went to answer it. A moment later, he returned.

"That was the moderator," he said. "We're meeting in fifteen minutes. You stay here with Bobby and I'll see you when I get back." Harris tipped his head and Connie, then at Bobby, and headed for the elevator.

"Nothing's going to happen for a while," Bobby said. "I'll call you if someone starts chatting. Why don't you go check out the scenery?"

135

Connie nodded, and went over to the curtain. She pulled it back and realized that there was a glass door with a balcony on the other side. She pulled it open and stepped out, gasping as she looked at the view beneath her.

It was early evening, and the sun was just going down in the west. The rays of the sun lit up the Danube River like diamonds, as Connie looked out across the water. As she watched, the lights began to appear, and one by one, the buildings across the river lit up and began to glow in the steadily growing gloom. She could see St. Stephan's Basilica off to the north, and Buda Castle off to the west with the famous Szechnyl Chain Bridge in the distance crossing the Danube. The river turned from green, to amber, to black.

Connie bit her lip, finding it hard to realize that 24 hours before she had been on the other side of the world, in boring old Texas. What would her sister Maddie, the world traveler, say if she could see her right now? And then she realized that she could never tell her sister what she was doing. Not only would it put people in danger, her sister included, but it would risk the success of every mission they had planned. She had already crossed that bridge, and now she was a Heretic. She couldn't go back and wouldn't if she could.

"Okay," she heard Bobby calling from the suite. She went back in the glass doors and closed them behind her. She joined Bobby in front of a bank of flatscreen monitors in the bedroom. Six screens were showing various views of three different hotel rooms. Two more were directed at the conference room where Harris was meeting.

"Find something?" she asked.

"Look at that," he said, pointing at the one in the upper right. It was in the British team's hotel suite. "Right there."

"What am I looking at?" The screen showed a suitcase with the lid opened and a red folder inside. On the outside was stamped a very large, gold **𝒱**.

"Okay, so he has a V on that folder," Connie said, stretching. "So what?"

"Harris has me doing a lot of research on this group of billionaires called the Consortium. They're the ones who officially hired the hit teams who killed our friends. It seems that the Consortium was recently visited—and taken over by someone who called himself Veritas."

"V for Veritas?" Connie said, yawning. "Makes sense. 'Course it could mean Victory, or Volvo, or Vaseline too. Kind of ironic though. Veritas is Latin for truth."

There was a buzz, and Bobby reached for a headset on the table. He put it on.

"Yeah, boss," he said. There was a pause, and then Connie saw him write a name down on a pad. Anais Singleton.

"Got it. I'll look him up." He put the headphone down and turned to Connie.

"Harris is still in the meeting, but he heard the name 'Anais Singleton' whispered by the Italian team as he was passing by. Glad he was wired."

"Uh," Connie said, and Bobby turned to her.

"You know something about this Singleton guy?"

"You could say that," she said. She told him about Singleton's visit to the bookstore, his inquiries about the Heretics, and then his sponsorship of the conference.

"Creepy," Bobby said.

"Or it could be a coincidence," Connie said. She stared at Bobby and shook her head. "No, it isn't." Her eyes narrowed. "Could this Singleton guy be Veritas?"

"Well, if he has any kind of digital footprint, I'll find out," Bobby said. "You pay attention to the rooms, like Harris wants you to, and I'll do some digging."

Connie nodded. She stared at the three rooms. Only one of them, the Italian suite, had people in it. Two women were talking in it. She put on the headset and listened in.

Five minutes later, she was asleep. ⋎

137

15

Sisters

Connie stirred several hours later, the headset still on her ears and over her hair, her body leaning over the table with the monitors towering above her. She rubbed her face and looked around her, the darkness of the room making her realize that it was now night.

"Sleeping beauty awakens," Bobby said next to her. She turned and looked at him, sitting in his wheelchair, staring at the monitors. "Don't worry. Not much is happening."

"What time is it?" she asked sheepishly.

"About eight," Bobby said. "Harris came in about an hour ago. He's in the next room. He told me to let you sleep. I wanted to move you to a bed, but he thought it would wake you."

"I feel like an idiot," Connie said. "My first chance to do something worthwhile and I fall asleep."

"Don't feel that way," Connie heard Harris' voice behind her, and turned to see him coming in, dressed in a suit. "You needed the sleep. You would have missed things if you were that tired anyway." Harris turned toward Bobby. "Did you find out anything more on Anais Singleton?"

"Do bears sleep in the woods?" Bobby replied. He turned and ran his fingers over the keyboard in front of him. As Connie watched, a photo of the man who had visited her philosophy class appeared on the screen. Bobby continued his presentation.

"Anais Singleton, former MI-6 biochemist. Worked there in psy-ops for six years until disappearing three years ago. My sources tell me he was working on a modern-day version of the CIA's old Project MK-Ultra."

Connie and Harris looked at Bobby blankly, and Bobby shook his head.

"Seriously?" he said. "You guys don't remember your history? MK-Ultra was the CIA's attempt to use LSD for mind-control in the 1960s. They gave up on the experiments when several people went crazy, and their secret got out. Apparently, Singleton convinced MI-6 that he could get it to work. The problem was biochemical."

"Why did he leave?" Harris asked.

"They got a new director, who didn't like the ethics of the project and scrubbed it. Singleton left. Now he's popping up here and there, and suddenly he's a very popular guy."

"How popular?"

"He's apparently got the Consortium bankrolling him," Bobby said. "One of their members, Sir McArthur Henson, suddenly added Singleton's name to all of his financial accounts. He has total access to billions of euros. And Singleton's been seen in London with some very powerful people who think he's a pretty cool guy."

"What about this 'Veritas' name that he's going by?" Connie asked.

"Not sure about that," Bobby said. "It could be an organization, a code name, or a cult that he's trying to start. I'll keep researching that." He looked at Harris. "So have we decided that the British team is the one who betrayed us?"

Harris pressed his lips together tightly. "Circumstantial evidence. They have a binder that has the Veritas logo on it. But I overheard the Italians mention Singleton's name." He frowned. "The weekend isn't over yet. I'll keep pressing them, and you two keep looking over their shoulder."

Connie yawned and stretched. "And I promise to stay awake, boss. Honestly."

Harris chuckled. "You can't stay awake all the time. But there is some coffee in the other room if you need it." He looked at Bobby.

"You're authorized to hack British government files if you need to," he said. "I suspect that there's more to Singleton than meets the eye. In the meantime, I have a dinner engagement I need to be present at. In fact, all the teams will be there. It'll be the perfect time for you, Connie, to look for more evidence."

"Me?" Connie squeaked. "How?"

"I need you to go through the suites of our colleagues while I keep them occupied," Harris said. "This dinner should keep them out of the building for a couple of hours. Plenty of time for you to find anything incriminating."

"Uh," Connie said. "I'm not sure how I feel about breaking and entering. I didn't study that at UT. Plus, I think a college student from Texas wandering the halls would be pretty obvious."

"First, we have a housekeeping outfit for you," Bobby said. "That, plus your new language skills will help you fit right in. Second, we're not 'breaking in' if we have the keys. Thanks to my computer skills, and the wonders of magnetic locks, we have all the keys we need. Now you need to get your housekeeping clothes on."

Connie looked at Bobby and then at Harris. Harris tipped his head at Connie.

"Listen to your Uncle Bobby," Harris said. "He'll teach you a thing or two. And later, you and I need to have a conversation. Okay?"

* * *

Harris Borden had eaten all kinds of food through the years but had never acquired a taste for rich food. Tonight's dinner at the world-famous Onyx Restaurant was traditional fare featuring lángos (deep-fried flatbread), főzelék (thick vegetable stew), pörkölt (stew), Töltött Káposzta (stuffed cabbage leaves) and of course, goulash. For dessert, they had Dobos Torte, sponge cake layered with chocolate buttercream and topped with caramel. By the time they were done, everyone was talking about how rich and filling the dinner was and thanking Pastor Jacob Pinterich for his hospitality.

"Of course," he said in English. "It was horrible what happened in Salzburg two months ago. I felt we needed to make up for that terrible event tonight."

"Do you think that a good meal can make up for the death of ten fellow Christians?" Harris said loudly from the end of the table. Immediately the talking stopped, and the room grew quiet.

"I didn't...I didn't think....," Pastor Pinterich stammered.

"No, you didn't think," Harris said, his voice growling at them. "None of you did. That's the problem. We started all of this because you wanted something different. You saw what we were doing with the Heretics in America and wanted the same thing in your own countries. Until one of you—or more—decided that maybe the status quo was better after all. And you decided that the best way, the only way, to stop it was to act like Judas and betray the group. Collect your thirty pieces of silver and lead the chosen ones to be crucified."

There was a dead silence as the group looked at each other, then at Harris. Then at each other again. Finally, Pastor Edwardo Scalzi of Italy spoke up.

"But how do we learn who did this terrible thing? And what do we do once we have learned it?"

Harris looked the group over and spoke slowly, definitively.

"I know who did this," he said. "And we're all going to learn their name tonight. Then it'll be up to this group to decide what to do about it."

The group didn't respond but waited for Harris to speak again.

"We know that the attack was called by a group called the Consortium, what we used to call the Brotherhood of the Altar. They have been doing evil things behind the scenes for more than six hundred years. We've discovered that they are now led by a man named Anais Singleton. Perhaps a few have heard that name mentioned here."

The group looked at each other, and the Italian team especially began to look at each other. Finally, Scalzi spoke up.

"But that is impossible," Scalzi said. "We were given that name as an investor in a project that we're working on. We were told that he was a good, reliable man."

"Who told you this?" Harris asked.

"Pastor Pinterich did," Scalzi said. Some of the others began to mutter among themselves.

"Some of you may have also heard of an organization called Veritas," Harris said. "Veritas is in fact, also Anias Singleton."

This time it was the British team who became nervous and began talking among themselves. One held up his hand.

"I was sent a prospectus from Veritas right before we left on this trip," the pastor said. "I haven't had a chance to read it, and I don't know where it came from."

"It came from me." They all turned to see Pastor Pinterich standing at his seat at the table. "I sent the prospectus. I slipped the name to Pastor Scalzi."

Harris smiled thinly. "Surely you must have realized that either act would have gotten you caught."

Pinterich nodded. "I suppose I did. But it was what I was told to do."

"By whom?" Harris asked. "Singleton? Did he tell you to do these things?"

Pinterich stared at the group of men sitting around the table and tears came to his eyes.

"God forgive me," he said. He then reached for a steak knife that lay next to the platter in front of him. He turned the blade toward himself and drove it into his chest before anyone could stop him. Blood poured out over the table, and Pastor Pinterich collapsed onto the table.

"Someone call for a doctor!" Pastor Scalzi shouted.

Harris stared at the man, a man of God, who had just killed himself after having ten other people murdered.

* * *

Connie spent two hours dressed in hotel housekeeping clothes going through the rooms of the three teams from Great Britain, Italy, and France. The team from Hungary was located nearby, but since they weren't in the hotel, she didn't worry about them. At first, Connie was nervous about the work, and got uncomfortable going through the personal items of the people who were there, but after a while got used to the routine. Once, she was interrupted in the hallway by another housekeeping worker, who asked in Hungarian what she was doing. Connie responded awkwardly, but also in Hungarian, telling the worker that they were adding towels to the suites there.

That was the extent of the danger she got in. And when all was said and done, she discovered nothing. Connie looked for the folder with the stylized 𝒴 on the front of it, but apparently the person who had received it had taken it with them to the dinner.

When they got back to the penthouse, Bobby seemed agitated.

"What's wrong?" Connie asked.

"There's been a death," Bobby said. "Harris called and said they discovered who was behind the attacks. It was the pastor from Hungary, who admitted it, then killed himself."

"Whoa," Connie said. "Guess I had the easy job."

"Look, tomorrow we head home, but I'm sure you're beat," Bobby said to Connie. "Take the main bedroom here and get some sleep. We'll be fine in here."

"Harris said he wanted to talk to me, but I guess it can wait until tomorrow," Connie said. "As it is, I'm so tired I wouldn't probably remember it anyway." She waved her hand weakly. "See you guys tomorrow."

She headed into the master bedroom and closed the door behind her. She stripped off her housekeeping outfit and crawled into the king-sized bed. She was asleep seconds after her head hit the pillow.

She awoke with sunlight streaming through the curtains. She got up and showered and changed clothes. Then she joined the other two in the main area of the suite.

"Good morning," Bobby said. He sat at the framework where the bank of monitors had stood the night before. Most of the equipment was already packed, and he and Harris were watching BBC news in English on the large flatscreen TV anchored on the opposite wall.

"Morning," Connie said. "How is everyone this morning?"

"We're doing okay, considering the night we had," Harris said. "I don't sleep much, and I knew Bobby had an early flight out, so I broke down his equipment for him. He'll be heading out in a few minutes."

"That's too bad," Connie said. "I was hoping the three of us could do some sightseeing."

Bobby chuckled, and Harris frowned.

"You forget that someone still wants us dead," Harris said. "Until we know more, it's not safe for the three of us to be out in public together."

"Yeah, besides I'm not much of a sightseer anyway," Bobby said. "I prefer my RV for traveling. I'm looking forward to getting back to it and seeing some beautiful American sights. PeeWee is supposed to meet me in Miami and we're going to hit Key West."

"Sounds pretty cool," Connie said. "What about you, Harris? When is your flight?"

He smiled back at her and shrugged. "I'm here in Europe for the duration. I won't be flying anywhere. I think we have time for a nice breakfast and that talk I was referring to last night."

"My flight is in several hours," Connie said. "Sure, why not."

Connie and Harris said goodbye to Bobby, and they had porters come and haul the boxed equipment downstairs to the waiting vehicle for transportation to the airport. Connie hadn't really known Bobby very well before this, but now realized she was going to miss him. She wondered if it was not only because she enjoyed his company in the short time they had together, but also because he was another tie to the other members of the team she was no longer around. She hugged him one more time before he went through the door, and he was gone.

"Sad," Connie said, as she looked at the hotel door where Bobby had just left. "I miss everyone so much."

"I do too," Harris said. "But I know they're safer this way. And when it comes down to it, this will help them rely more on God than on each other. That's an important lesson to learn. One that I had to learn the hard way."

"So…when you said breakfast, you weren't talking about an actual restaurant, were you?" Connie said slowly.

Harris smiled and shook his head.

"Sorry," he said. "When this is all over with, I promise you I'll take you wherever you want to go. For now, you'll have to settle for a breakfast on our balcony. We'll order from the hotel kitchen and have it delivered. Then we can sit out here and talk."

Connie told Harris that she wanted a vegan breakfast, so they ordered egg substitutes, potatoes, fresh fruit, and tomatoes. She ordered orange juice to drink. Harris ordered the same. While he was on the phone ordering their breakfast, Connie watched the BBC news on TV, and was startled to see a photo of her sister, Dr. Madelyn Simms, at a conference in Moscow. She watched the captions and learned that Maddie had been brought there to speak about a recently discovered manuscript that was rumored to be part of the biblical canon.

"That's your sister, isn't it?" Harris said, as he hung up the phone.

"Yeah, it is," Connie said. "Off to become world famous again." She stared at the screen for a long time before turning to Harris. "You know, she tried to convince me to move back home so that I could be close to my parents. My father has been ill, and she wanted me there to help take care of him."

Harris blinked. "How do you feel about that?"

"I thought it was pretty underhanded of her," Connie said. "She gets to travel all over the world, leaving at a moment's notice. But I have to play the dutiful sister and take care of Daddy."

"Looks like neither one of you stayed home," Harris said quietly.

"No, we didn't," Connie said. "And I feel bad about that."

"Look, there's no easy answer here," Harris said. "You could call your sister and try to talk it out."

"I could," Connie said. "I've thought about that more than once. But she's got this idea that what I'm doing isn't important."

A knock came at the front door. Harris went to it, peeping through the peephole first, then answering the door. The bellhop brought in the tray of food, and Harris signed the bill. The bellhop left and Harris and Connie wheeled the food out onto the balcony.

"A little chilly," Harris said. "You might need a jacket."

"I'm fine," Connie said. "Let's eat."

They sat down at the small table on the balcony, and after Harris said the blessing, they began to eat.

"Just for argument's sake," Connie said, jabbing a tomato. "What would happen if I were to go home and visit my parents? Check up on them?"

Harris put down his fork and looked at her. "You know what kind of danger we're in here. Do you really want to put your parents, or your sister, in that same danger? Would they even understand?"

"No, I guess not," Connie said. She took another bite of her food, and then suddenly realized that she was crying. She dropped her fork and picked up her napkin and put it to her eyes. The tears gushed from her eyes, and the crying turned into sobs.

"I never realized how much I hate tomatoes," she muttered to herself, still looking down. "They're too red. The color of blood. I mean, what was God thinking when He created them? Morbid if you ask me."

Harris didn't say anything in return.

"Daddy has a vegetable garden outside the kitchen," she continued. "Every year he raises tomatoes. The plants grow six feet tall. Mama loves cherry tomatoes. He loves to pick them when they are sweet and pop them in her mouth. She acts like she hates it, but they both laugh about it."

Harris sat patiently waiting as she continued crying for several minutes. He didn't put his arms around her but just waited. Finally, the sniffling died down, and she looked up at him.

"Are you all right?" he asked.

She nodded. "Better. I understand, Harris. But it's hard."

Harris sighed. "Connie, that's why I wanted to have this talk with you. Alone. The Heretics are entering a new phase. There will be times when we work together, such as what we did this weekend. But much of what we will be doing will be alone and separate. And extremely dangerous. It's important that each of us learn to lean on God rather than ourselves or each other. It's critical. And I see you as an important part of our plans going forward."

Connie looked up, her eyes still red. "Me? What do you expect me to do?"

"Isn't it obvious?" Harris said. "I'm training you to be one of our leaders. One of these days I won't be around. Perhaps Josh and Taupe won't be around either. And the Heretics will be looking to you as their leader."

Connie stared at Harris, scarcely believing what she was hearing. Then she shook her head.

"I...I could never be like you, Harris," she said. "No way."

Harris smiled. "That's fine. Just be Connie. Trust God and be Connie." 𝒱

16

Bulletproof

Georgetown, Maryland
That Same Night

Ruth and Douglas Washington were just wrapping things up at the office of the Center for Concerned Studies—the place where nothing ever happened—when she got a familiar text from an unfamiliar number. It consisted of simply one word: *Dragonsreach*.

The word was enough. It told her who it was, and where and when he wanted to meet. She hesitated, and Douglas caught the hesitation. He shrugged.

"Look, I'll catch a cab home," he said. "You stay and take care of business." He tossed his car keys to her. She caught them and nodded.

She knew that the word Dragonsreach was just another location for her to connect with her brother in the online role-playing game The Elder Scrolls Online. She logged on via her laptop and entered the world via her catlike Khajit thief, Katara. In another minute, she was headed for Dragonsreach, the jarl's castle that overlooked the city of Whiterun. She ran through the wooden castle, with NPC's making comments to her as she moved past them. If she knew her brother, he would want somewhere relatively quiet—and picturesque.

She found Josh's tall blonde Nord warrior Habermas, dressed in his black armor, standing in the sunshine overlooking the valley in the massive entryway where each of them had captured the famous dragon Odahviing. Today there was only the tall warrior, her brother.

"Hello, stranger," she purred as she came up to him. "Aren't you afraid Sparky is going to overhear us?"

"Well, if the NSA has discovered this link as he says they have, then probably nothing's safe," Habermas/Josh said. "How are things at your end?"

"Oh, you know, pretty boring," she said. "Can't say much, but we are making some progress."

"That's good," the warrior said. "Pretty much the same here. We have a meeting scheduled for tomorrow with the new guard, the ones that call themselves The Ronin. Bikers. Hard dudes."

"You be careful," Ruth/Katara said. "You're not a young man anymore."

Josh chuckled. "I've still got a few tricks up my sleeve," he said. "And God is still in charge."

"Speaking of which, I know you didn't call this meeting to just check on me. What's up?"

"I ran off without giving Adam the information he needs to keep the bookstore running. Bank stuff."

"Is it a lot? You want to Dropbox it to me?" Ruth said. "I'm trying to decide the safest way to do this if Big Brother is listening, which we can assume he is."

"No, my messages on my phone are encrypted so I can send them at least once. I'll send it to you. You're the most visible of all of us, so if you don't mind, I'll use you as a conduit for this. I don't think I'll try a second time. I'm pretty secure where I am, but twice is probably asking for trouble."

"Got it," Ruth said. "Okay, then I'll wait for the information and get it to Adam. Take care of yourself. You're in my prayers."

"And you're in mine," Josh said. "Love you, Sis."

* * *

New York City
Police Commissioners Meeting

"I know that you're used to following a pretty tight schedule and formal agenda at these meetings," Hugh Watson, police commissioner from Chicago said to the group of thirty men and women who were seated in the hall. "But I hope you'll indulge me this afternoon. For I have had the opportunity to meet a unique person who I believe has something to share with us. He brings to this group a promise of hope and unity for not only our nation, but for our world. Ladies and Gentlemen, fellow police commissioners, I give you Dr. Anais Singleton!"

The slight man in the suit stood to polite applause, with most of those in the audience not sure exactly what to expect from this unknown man. He looked down at the podium in front of him, scratched the side of his nose, then looked up at the people there. They were all leaders in law enforcement from around the United States. Every major city was represented here. And now he would control them.

As he opened his mouth to speak, a strange, sweet smell permeated the room.

* * *

Bergstrom Intl. Airport, Austin
The Next Morning

Connie didn't remember much on the trip back from Budapest. She sleepwalked through the Frankfurt connection and through her connection at Dallas-Fort Worth Airport. When she was in the air, she just slept. Fortunately, she had access to a first-class private waiting area in Frankfurt and Dallas, so she found a comfortable chair and slept there as well. Nineteen hours later she was standing on the curb outside baggage claim, wearing her denim "Eat at Joe's" jacket, waving for Adam as he drove up in his BMW.

"Hi," she gushed. "Glad to go. More glad to get home."

"Any chance of you telling me where you were?" Adam asked. "Of course, considering the hasty way you've been cramming Hungarian into your repertoire, I can take a pretty good guess."

Connie shrugged. "Guessing's free, and probably on target. But I'm not telling. Even though I will tell you that it was *gorgeous*."

Adam chuckled. "Actually, I've been there, so yeah, I know. But I'm glad you're back."

Connie stared at Adam as he started up the car and pulled out into traffic.

"So," she said cautiously. "Any news about our thirteen year old?"

Adam sighed. "Well, he was more convincing than you or I would have been. He got accepted into the Mystics."

"Really," Connie said. "How do you know?"

"He left a message on the trash can behind the bookstore this morning. The kid is more stealthy than we give him credit for."

"He still scares me," Connie said. "And are you going to want it on your conscience if he gets hurt?"

"No, of course not," Adam said. "But there's not a heck of a lot we can do right now. Speaking of getting hurt…" He paused and looked at Connie.

"What?" Connie said. "Now you're scaring me."

"That detective that got you out of jail that one time? I think his name is Shapiro. He came by looking for you. He left a message. Said to tell you that Selah White has been released from prison."

Cold chills went down Connie's back. She stared at Adam silently as if she didn't believe what she had just heard.

"Yeah, I thought that would get your attention," Adam said. "He thought so too. He said if you hear or see anything of her sniffing around, contact him and they'll get a restraining order put out on her."

Connie was silent for a long while, staring at the road ahead of them. Then she spoke.

"Where's my bo staff? The one I left with you?"

"What, that stick? Why do you need that?"

"I need it because I need it," Connie said. "And it's not a stick, it's a weapon."

"Since when have you started carrying weapons?"

"Since our enemies have started multiplying around us," Connie said, mostly to herself. "Now where is it?"

"Relax. It's in the trunk." Adam paused. "You do realize that Selah White is my aunt."

"That didn't stop her from kidnapping and trying to kill me," Connie said. "Pardon me for not being too cordial if she shows up."

They arrived half an hour later, and after Connie dropped her bag off at the dorm, she went with Adam over to the bookstore to check on Miracle.

"With Crash gone, it's been hard to keep the bookstore going and feed and walk this monster every day," Adam said.

"He's no monster," Connie said, rubbing the big dog's head and neck. "Although I will have to admit he's gotten huge while I was gone." The black and brown puppy was almost full grown and well over a hundred pounds.

"And you were only gone, what, three days?" Adam said. "I'm not sure this apartment is going to be big enough for him soon."

"Well, I will take over until Crash is back," Connie said. "I'll take him for a walk this evening. How are we doing on food?"

"He's already gone through two forty-pound bags," Adam said. "And remember your promise about poop patrol? Well, I'm holding you to it."

"Yes, understood," Connie said. "I'm on it." She picked up a scoop and bucket and began cleaning up around the apartment. A moment later, she got the chain leash off the ring on the wall and hooked it to Miracle's collar.

"Come on, baby," she said. "Let's take it out to the alley." She grabbed her bo staff as she stepped out the door. Five minutes later, they were back, and Connie discovered that Adam was on his laptop talking to Ruth via Facetime.

"Hi, Ruth," Connie said, waving over Adam's shoulder. "I won't ask you where you are, since that kind of information seems to be secret these days. But how are you doing?"

Ruth laughed. "I'm one of the few on the team whose location isn't secret. I'm in Georgetown, Maryland, just outside Washington, D.C. Douglas and I are doing some research for the government."

"Well, we're glad you called," Connie said. "We miss everyone."

"Yeah, well, I'm calling because I was told you need banking information for the bookstore. I talked to Josh and he told me to check in on you two."

"Glad Josh is concerned. We had a break in about a week ago and three goons came in and stole Josh's laptop. But everything is encrypted. Sorry."

"Well, it's a good thing I'm calling then," Ruth said. "Let me send you the information. Are you on a VPN there?"

"Yes, I finally discovered it after Josh's computer got stolen. I've got my computer up on it and it's encrypted. So feel free to send the banking information."

"Ruth, we need to tell you about someone who's been snooping around here," Connie said. "He's also shown up on Harris' radar. He's definitely a person of interest."

"Oh?"

"Yes, his name is Anais Singleton," Connie said. "He's a polite, unassuming Brit, and seems to be very nice. But according to Harris and Bobby, he may be behind everything that's happening. Also be aware of the name Veritas."

"What is Veritas?" Adam asked.

"Don't know for sure," Connie said. "Could be an organization, or a password. But Singleton has been using it as his own identification."

"Got it," Ruth said. "We're mingling with a lot of government types here. Let's see if either name rings a bell. At the same time, let's all be extra careful."

"Understood," Connie said.

"Ruth," Adam said. "Did Josh give any instructions as to what I should do with the bookstore until he gets back?"

Ruth bit her lip. "I don't think you understand, Adam. It's not his intention to ever come back. He's signed all the papers for the bookstore over to you. I'll send you a copy. The bookstore is yours."

Adam's mouth dropped open.

"Me? What do I know about running a bookstore?"

Ruth laughed. "You know more than Josh did when he started it. Besides, who else would you suggest take the store over?"

Adam didn't have an answer but looked at Ruth for a long moment before Ruth spoke again.

"Remember, kids, that the store is just a tool," Ruth said. "Our job goes far beyond selling books. We're saving souls and saving lives. The situation we're in isn't ideal, but we believe in the two of you. Harris saw something in you when he was here. He still sees it." She hesitated as Ruth looked at Connie. "And Connie, I'm glad to see you're still wearing that jacket. Keep it close." She looked over her shoulder, as if someone else had come into the room.

"Look, I've got to go," she said. "But call me if you need to."

They disconnected from Facetime and stared at each other. Both Connie and Adam seemed lost.

"I own a bookstore," Adam muttered to himself. "What would my dad think?"

"A self-made businessman without having to touch his daddy's money," Connie agreed. "How does that make you feel?"

Adam grinned. "Actually, pretty good. I may not be in school, but this bookstore keeps me plenty busy. And if I am going to take this business seriously...." He was interrupted by a whine/howl from Miracle. "If I am going to take this business seriously, it has to stop smelling like a kennel. My first order of business is that guy needs a new home, starting tomorrow."

Connie nodded. "Not sure how we'll swing it, but yeah, I agree. Miracle is way too big to be living in a little apartment. He needs a farm somewhere where he can roam. Not sure where I'll find such a place, but maybe God has some ideas. We'll keep praying about it."

She looked over her shoulder at Miracle.

"In the meantime, I think our Miracle is telling us that he needs to make a visit outside again." She sighed. "Yes, he definitely needs a big yard somewhere."

She grabbed the leash again and called for Miracle. The big dog bounded to her, and the wooden floorboards under him creaked and groaned with the strain.

"Okay, while you take care of him, I suddenly remembered I have a bookstore to run," Adam said.

Connie walked Miracle out into the alley, waiting for him to do his duty. But like most dogs, he was more interested in sniffing the neighborhood than getting down to business. Ten minutes later, he was still sniffing papers at the end of the alley.

"Seriously?" Connie said to Miracle. "Can you just pick a place and take care of things? It's getting late here, dog."

Miracle looked up at her as if she had said something funny and wagged his stubby tail. Then he turned toward the entrance of the alley and froze. A moment later, he began to growl. Connie turned to look and saw three big men coming out of the darkness. Immediately she wondered if they were the same men who had attacked Adam in the bookstore. Then she realized another thing: she had left her bo staff in the apartment.

"Are you Connie Simescu?" the one in the front asked.

She thought back several months to a fight in the parking lot of a bar where she had been asked the same question. When she had said Yes, the big man had reached out and tried to drag her off by the hair. She had only been rescued by Taupe and Josh, and the prompt arrival of the police.

"Are you Connie Simescu?" the man repeated.

"*Miért kérdezed?*" she asked him in Hungarian.

Miracle's growl became a bark. The man in front nodded to the other two.

"That's her," he said. "Take her."

Connie had no intention of letting Miracle go to attack the men in front of her, but holding a hundred-pound Rottweiler when it is trying to protect its master was something she was not prepared to do. Miracle jerked the leash right out of Connie's hands. A second later, he was on top of the man in front. He hit the man like a Houston Texans linebacker and the man went down. The two men behind him hesitated, and Connie took that moment to try to decide what to do.

Her first instinct was to run, but she couldn't leave Miracle behind. She looked around her and saw a four-foot piece of one-inch galvanized steel pipe lying at her feet. She reached for it, and as she raised it, one of the men was on her. She whipped the pipe around to try and hit him in the side of the head, but he raised his arm and deflected the blow.

"Jesus, help me," she whispered, as the man reached for the pipe. She pulled it back out of his reach, then rammed it into his midsection. The man folded in front of her.

She heard a yelp and saw that the third man had come to the rescue of the leader who had been attacked by Miracle. He had pulled a blade from his pocket and was jabbing it into the ribs of the dog. As she watched, the blade hit Miracle a second time.

"No!" she shouted. She swung the galvanized pipe over her head and brought it down on the head and shoulders of the man attacking her. He collapsed to the ground. She wanted to hit him again and again to make sure he stayed down, but her first concern was for Miracle.

"Get off him," Connie barked at them. "Leave my dog alone."

Miracle, despite being bloody and stabbed several times, had turned his attention to the man with the knife. He grabbed the arm with the knife, and as Connie watched, the knife dropped out of his hand. The man then stood and staggered backward. Then he turned and ran. Connie watched Miracle struggle to his feet, then he started to run after the man.

"Miracle!" Connie said, running after Miracle as he bounded toward the alley's exit. "No, come back. Miracle, come back."

She ran past the man on the ground and looked for Miracle in the dark. A moment later, she heard the click of a hammer being pulled back on a pistol.

"Say goodbye," the man said.

Connie heard an explosion and felt a sledgehammer blow hitting her in the back, followed by a sharp pain like a knife. She fell face down into a puddle of water and lay still. 𝒴

17

Diamonds and Black Jesus

East Los Angeles

Josh and Pastor Escobar spent the afternoon cleaning up the Mission where the Children of God had met years before. They pulled boards loose that covered the windows, swept floors and cobwebs from the ceiling, fixed wiring and plumbing, and repaired what they could on the stairs outside the small building.

"You know, this place is going to take a lot more than two white collar guys and a couple of brooms to get started again," Pastor Escobar said. He paused and wiped the sweat from his forehead. "I'm not proud, but it's been a while since I've done this kind of work."

"This place holds a lot of memories for me," Josh said, pausing to look up from his broom. "The old couple who ran it, Ma and Pa Smith we used to call them, they were like family. And I keep praying that God will lead someone else here to take charge." He paused. "I have my wishes here, and I'm assuming you do too, but they don't mean anything if it's not what God wants."

Pastor Escobar grinned. "Yeah, He's reminding me of that. I was getting a little too comfortable where I'm at, I'll have to admit. And then He sent you to remind me where I came from." Rico looked past Josh out the open door. Josh turned and saw the two young teenage boys from a few doors down who had been working on their car, followed by Herman, their father.

"*Hola*," the older man said. "Thought you could use some help. That and something to drink. Brought some beers, and if that's not something you go for, I've got some Cokes as well."

Rico grinned. "Thanks, Herman." He smiled and held out his hand and Herman shook it. Josh shook the hands of the two teenagers, then handed them brooms.

"Looks like this place could use a coat of paint," Herman said, looking up at the ceiling, then at the other rooms. "The whole place. I can get a team over here in a couple of days."

"It could use a total makeover, that's for sure," Pastor Escobar said. "I'm thinking I need to take this project to my church board as an outreach."

Josh grinned. "Now we're talking. This needs to be a labor of love from a lot of people, not just one or two. And even if the neighborhood has changed, there are still a lot of needs around here. Things that this center can help with."

As he spoke, the sound of motorcycles grew louder. One, then several Harleys appeared outside the open front door of the Mission. The two teen boys stopped sweeping and looked at each other, a worried expression covering their faces. Josh looked at Pastor Escobar as they heard the booted steps of several men approach from outside. A moment later, a large tattooed Hispanic man in his 20s wearing black leathers and wrap-around sunglasses came in the door, followed by three more.

The man in front stood there silently for a long moment, just looking at the room and what they were doing. Finally, he spoke, his voice coming out a deep growl.

"I'm Viper. You opening the Mission up again?"

"Thinking about it," Pastor Escobar said. "It used to do good things for this neighborhood. It could again."

Viper nodded slightly. "I agree. My *abuela* learned to speak English here and the Mission helped her get her citizenship." He looked around at the dusty room. "This place is a mess. You need help. We'll send some guys over."

Viper turned to go and Josh raised his hand to stop him. The man raised his eyebrow, unused to people stopping him when he set his mind to doing something.

"Do you remember the people who used to run this place?" Josh asked him. "A nice old couple named Ma and Pa Smith?"

159

Viper hesitated and his features softened. "Yeah, I remember them. He had kind eyes. She gave me candy."

"We need someone to run this place," Josh said. "Someone like them."

Viper thought for a moment, then nodded. Then he turned and left.

"That was just what we need," Herman said sarcastically, looking out the door after they left. "Those *alborotadores* getting involved will ruin everything. They'll scare the whole community away."

"No," Pastor Escobar said, shaking his head. "No, this is a gift from God. Each of those young men was born and raised in this neighborhood." He looked up and reached up to slap Herman on the shoulder. "Just like you and me, Herman. They are demonstrating that they do really care what happens here, just as we did all those years ago when we were the Ronin."

They turned and looked at the two teen boys, their eyes big.

"What," Pastor Escobar said. "Your father never told you that we were gangbangers together?" Pastor Escobar laughed, and then Herman laughed with him.

"More like rebels without a clue," Herman said.

Josh watched the two men laugh together and smiled as he looked out the doorway. Yes, it was all coming together. Why then, did he still feel uneasy?

* * *

South Chicago

Taupe looked around her at the meeting hall in the Hyatt Regency Hotel. The entire building had been bought out for the day, and if it hadn't, the typical customers probably wouldn't have wanted to come and use the hotel anyway, knowing who was meeting in the main hall.

Gone were the days where gang leaders skulked around in broken down tenements and seedy apartments, afraid of being seen by the authorities. Most of the people coming today had been arrested and imprisoned at least once, and the police knew exactly who they were. Chances are, the police had already infiltrated several of their clubs, and there was the distinct chance that the room was bugged. But Three Peat and Taupe didn't care. What they had to say would soon be public information anyway.

Taupe sat at the front table with Three Peat, his sister on the other side of him. Taupe noticed that his lieutenants were busy at the door, making sure nobody came in armed. A few grumbled and complained, but eventually went along with the protocol. Finally, everyone was seated.

The tables were set up in a square, with the four major gangs of South Chicago represented on each side of the square with Three Peat and his delegation from The Lords at the head of the table. The other three gangs represented were The Disciples, the Cobras, and the Hustlers.

"Okay, now I don't wanna waste your time," Three Peat said to the leaders of the other groups. "We been trying to have this meeting forever, and I thank you for being here. The cops been trying to promote this gang war between us, and it's time it stopped."

"What, you here to surrender already?" Shogun, the leader of the Disciples said loudly. One of the Hustlers laughed with him, then cut it off when he realized that no one else was laughing.

"This got nothin' to do with our gangs or our territory," Three Peat said. "This got to do with how our community been treated and how we treating our community."

"Oh, come on, Three Peat," Moss, the leader of the Cobras spoke up. "We ain't no bleeding hearts bunch of nuns. We bad muthers. Or at least the Cobras are."

"Yeah. Right," Three Peat said quietly. "Go ahead, Moss, trying to prove how bad you is. Seems like we is always having to prove it to someone. Why is that? Why we always having to prove it? Why don't people just believe it? Because we ain't doing what we need to be doing. Listen, we has the power to change lives here. Our mothers. Our sisters. Our children. What you done for your children lately?"

Moss spoke up again. "What, you suddenly got religion, Three Peat? Why you caring about other people all of a sudden?"

"Why not?" Three Peat said, standing up. "Why not? In 1969, look what the Black Panthers done in the city of Oakland for the Black brothers and sisters there when no one else cared. Did anyone question whether they was bad or not? They offered free breakfasts for children. They opened health clinics. They educated their people. What wrong with that?"

Moss shook his head. "This is a bunch of crap."

Shogun shook his head. "No, he's right. When was the last time the white man did anything for you? When was the last time the city came and took care of your community? It's up to us to take care of our own."

Three Peat smiled thinly. "One gang has a little power. Four gangs, covering all of South Chicago, working together? When has that ever happened before? What kind of power is that?"

At that comment, the others began to mutter in agreement. Three Peat added another statement.

"And to answer your question, Moss, yes. I've found religion. I've found the Black Jesus."

* * *

The Alley Behind Reborn Bookstore
Downtown Austin

Connie opened her eyes to see Detective Shapiro looking at her. It was night, and she realized that she was still lying on the cobblestones in the alleyway behind the bookstore.

"Lie still," Detective Shapiro said. "I've called for an ambulance."

"I'm all right," Connie said, trying to sit up, then groaned as pain shot through her side and back. "Oww, that hurts." She lay back down.

"It should. You've been shot," Detective Shapiro said. "In fact, you should be dead. What saved you was that it was apparently a small caliber bullet, probably a 22." He felt her jacket between his finger and thumb. "Where'd you get this jacket?"

"A friend gave it to me," Connie said. She rolled over and again tried to sit up, this time moaning but successful.

"I told you to lie still," Shapiro said. "They'll need to check you out." She heard sirens coming and Shapiro looked behind him as the ambulance pulled up to the entrance. "Looks like your friend saved your life."

"Guess so," Connie said, then whispered. "Thanks, Ruth."

The paramedics walked over to Shapiro, who gestured to Connie.

"She won't lie down, guys," he said. "What can I say."

"I'm all right," Connie said. "Just gonna have a heckova bruise."

"Let me see that," the first paramedic said, pulling her coat and blouse up and looking at her back where the bullet had hit. The other began taking vitals. "Yeah, I wouldn't doubt that you've at least cracked a rib here, but I don't think it's broken. No internal injuries that I can tell."

"See," Connie said to Shapiro. "Now can I go?"

"You sure you don't want a trip to the hospital to be checked out?" the paramedic asked her.

"I'm sure," Connie said. "But thanks."

Shapiro turned to Connie.

"Listen, I'd really rather you go with these guys, but it's up to you," he said. "I'll take care of this, and then we need to talk. So don't go anywhere."

Connie watched as Detective Shapiro signed some paperwork with the paramedics, then she signed a form herself signifying release from treatment. The paramedics packed up and got in their ambulance and drove away. Detective Shapiro returned to Connie.

He spent the next ten minutes having Connie tell him about the incident with Miracle and the three men. She described them in detail and emphasized that she thought they were the same men who had broken into the bookstore and attacked Adam some time before.

"Do you know why they attacked you?" Shapiro asked. "Or dare I even ask?"

"Sure, you can ask," Connie said. "But I'm not sure I can give you an answer you'll like, or even write down. The real answer is, I just don't know."

"It's a good thing I came across you," he said. "Let me drive you back to the dorm."

"I was walking my dog," she said, wincing as she tried to look around her. "Big rottweiler. I've got to find him. He lives at the bookstore."

"What kind of dog lives at a bookstore?" Shapiro asked. "Besides, there was no dog when I arrived. Look, you're in no shape to go looking for a lost dog. Let me take you home. I'll put out a bulletin on the dog and let your boyfriend at the bookstore know what happened. Like I said, it's a good thing I came by."

"Yeah, were you stalking me?" Connie said, starting to limp toward his car. "'Course in a case like this, that might be a good thing."

"No, I was in the neighborhood and thought I'd come by and check on you," Shapiro said. "Serendipity."

"Or maybe God using you," Connie suggested. They got in and he started up the engine. A moment later they were headed down Guadalupe toward the dorm.

Shapiro shrugged. "Maybe. Tell me who that friend was who gave you that jacket."

"Ruth Washington," Connie said. "I worked for her husband. He was an adjunct professor here at UT."

"Was?" Shapiro asked. "Where is he now?"

"Washington D.C., I think," Connie said. "He's a former congressman, and I think they got called back to do some government work."

"Well, that's an awfully fancy jacket," Shapiro said. "How did she know you'd get shot in that alleyway?"

"Beats me," Connie said. "But I'm glad she did."

"Well, so am I," Shapiro said. "I've had to rescue you too many times to lose you now."

"Thanks," Connie said. "I don't want to lose me either. But like I said before, I think God had something to do with it as well."

"Maybe so, Connie. Maybe so."

After Detective Shapiro let her out at the dorm, Connie thought about the jacket as well. What must it be made of to stop a bullet like that, yet be light enough for her to wear it casually like she did? When she was finally alone in her room, she took the jacket off and looked at it more closely.

There, on the right side, just below the shoulder blade in the back was a small mark where she was sure the bullet had hit her. In fact, the material was frayed there, and she could see that beneath the blue denim fabric was a fine mesh of what looked like many layers of silk. It must have been that which had stopped the bullet, she thought. And then she saw something else.

Among all the silver sequins that spelled out "Eat at Joe's" on the back of the jacket, one that was nearest the spot of the gunshot had come loose. She pulled on it and it came off in her hand. She held it up to the light and looked at it.

It was a small diamond.

Connie was stiff and sore the next morning when she got up, but she took a hot shower and loaded up on Ibuprofen and went to classes. *So this is the life of a Heretic*, she thought to herself as she limped through the hallway. *That's what happens when you get what you asked for.*

The philosophy class was caught up in the buzz of the upcoming conference, and students were talking about it not only in the classroom, but in the hallway as well. Connie heard one student say that they had been forced to move from one smaller lecture hall to a larger performance hall due to expected attendance. The Bates Recital Hall was on the far side of campus, but it held seven hundred people.

The thought of that made her nervous, and she thought to herself, *what have I done?* With everything else going on in her life, did she really need to be speaking for a philosophy conference? At the same time, in the back of her mind, she wondered if the conference was God working His will out for her.

Lord, she prayed. *I have no idea what I am doing. But I am in your hands. Give me the words and the actions I need to do the right thing.*

And then she thought about Crash. He was still gone, somewhere in the middle of the Mystics, probably at the home of that retired professor. It wasn't a safe place for anyone to be, much less a thirteen year old.

She was still thinking about him that afternoon when she walked back over to the bookstore. By that time her body had loosened up enough that she didn't limp quite so badly, even though it still hurt when she inhaled, coughed, or laughed.

Adam was at the front desk, and surprisingly, was helping a customer, Mrs. Sandoval, who came in once a week or so. Connie came in the doorway and waited patiently at a distance while Mrs. Sandoval dug through her purse for change, then paid Adam for the paperback that she was purchasing.

"Thanks for coming in," Adam told her, and the older lady nodded and left.

"Hey," Adam said to Connie. "How's it going?"

"We need to talk about Crash," Connie said. "What are we going to do about him?"

Adam inhaled and then let it out forcefully.

"Well, first of all, we need to locate him," he said. "Is he over at their mission or is he at Prof. Hughes' house?"

"Which means we need to do some scouting," Connie said. "The very thing he was supposed to do." She shook her head.

"Yeah, I know," Adam said. "Kids these days. Look, one of us needs to visit their mission and see if there's any sign of him. If he isn't there, then we will know he's at the professor's home."

"Will we?" Connie said. "These are the same people who kidnapped me and two other girls and locked us up in a dungeon. They were planning on *sacrificing* us, Adam. Do you see why the whole thing makes me nervous?"

"How about this?" Adam said. "Now that we know my aunt is out of prison and in town, how about I give her a call and see if she has seen him?"

Connie raised an eyebrow. "You really want to cross that bridge? She was the one that was responsible for my kidnapping. I don't know if she knows that we are together, but…no."

They stood and stared at each other, out of answers for the moment.

"I hate to say it, but maybe I need to call Detective Shapiro," Connie said. "There's a risk that Crash will end up in Child Protective Services, but at this point, we probably need to take that risk."

"I think that's a bad idea."

The voice came from above them. Connie and Adam turned to see Crash standing on the stairs leading up to the apartment. He was eating a bag of Takis.

"Hey guys," he said casually. "What's happening?"

18

End of the Line

Connie was speechless. Adam's mouth dropped open. But Crash acted as if he'd just woken up from a nap and wanted to catch up on the latest gossip. He was still dressed in the same Spiderman T-shirt that he had been wearing when he disappeared as well as a pair of holey jeans and his worn Converse All-Stars. By the time Connie and Adam had recovered, Crash had finished his bag of Takis. He crumpled the bag and held it out in front of him, looking for the nearest waste basket.

"Where's Miracle, by the way?" he asked. "I didn't see him upstairs."

Adam looked at Connie. "Yeah, your cop friend came by and told me that Miracle was missing, but he was kind of cryptic as to why. What happened?"

Connie suddenly realized that she would need to tell both of them what had happened.

"Those guys who attacked you here? They visited us in the alley last night."

"Are you all right?" Adam asked.

"Miracle? Is he all right?" Crash's voice raised in pitch and in volume.

"Yeah, I'm okay," Connie said, deciding to skip the part where she got shot. "But Miracle got hurt, and then chased one of them off. By the time it was all over, he had run out onto Guadalupe and down the street."

"We've got to go find him!" Crash said, a note of panic in his voice. "He could be hurt somewhere."

"We will," Adam said. "He's a big dog. Chances are, the Humane Society picked him up. Or someone rescued him. When dogs get injured, they panic and run away sometimes. Let him settle down, and maybe he'll be back at our doorstep. I'll make some calls."

"What about you?" Connie said, looking at Crash. "You've been gone a week. Where were you and what did you learn? We've been worried about you."

"Aww, I'm touched," Crash said. "I tried to tell you, I'm an alley cat. I always land on my feet. I was over at the Mystic Palace—that's what they call their shelter—for most of that time, but I helped at Dr. Hughes' house too. It's funny how little attention they pay to thirteen year olds, especially when I'm sweeping or mopping or doing dishes. I got a lot of housekeeping done, and in the meantime, I overheard a lot of what's going on."

"So…what *is* going on?" Adam asked.

"Not very much that's interesting. There was some arguing between those in charge," Crash said. "Some of them were upset because they were used to doing things their own way. But this pretty lady with white hair showed up and told everyone that she was in charge now."

Connie and Adam looked at each other. *Selah White*, they thought together.

"Funny thing was, the way she talked, I got the impression that she was getting her orders from somewhere else. They really aren't doing anything different than they were before, but it's like they're waiting for something big to happen. When that happens, then they'll make big changes."

Adam looked at Crash. "Did you happen to hear the name Anais Singleton while you were there?"

"Or Veritas?" Connie added.

Crash shook his head. "I would have stayed longer, but I made friends with a girl named Marita. She gave me this to give to you. It sounded urgent. That's why I left." He pulled a folded-up note from his pants pocket and gave it to Connie. She unfolded it and read it:

So many apologies to make. So many things I wish I could have told you. I want you to know that it's not your fault. God can never forgive me for all that I've done, and I can't live with my mistake. I'm going back to where we met. Tonight. I love you and hope that you, my sister, will forgive me. –M.

Connie put the note down and looked at Crash.

"How did she look when she gave you this note?" she asked.

"Sad," he said. "She always looked sad."

* * *

Russell Senate Office Building
Washington, D.C.

"After all the cloak and dagger for so long, I'm surprised that you're willing to meet with me face-to-face like this," Douglas Washington said to Senator Albert Bemis as he sat behind his desk in the expansive office.

Bemis shrugged. "That was then, this is now. In the beginning, I wanted to make sure that you were invited to the right parties and were viewed as impartial in your investigations. Fact is, I'm surprised you didn't bring your wife along as well." Senator Bemis stood up and walked over to the liquor cabinet and started to pour himself a drink. "Can I get you anything?"

"No thanks," Douglas said. "Things were pretty slow to begin with, but with Ruth's persistence and the fact that I still know a lot of people, we got invited to quite a few parties. Maybe even more than we really wanted."

"Great, great," Senator Bemis said. "So, do you have a list yet?"

"A preliminary list," Douglas said. "We have a few names that fall in the definitely corrupt category, with several others that line up in lesser degrees after them."

Senator Bemis held out his hand, and after a slight hesitation, Douglas reached into his briefcase and pulled out a folder. He gave it to the senator, who sat down at his desk. Bemis read through the list slowly. Then he reached for a pen and began scribbling on the page.

"What are you doing?" Douglas said.

"Son, you're doing a great thing here," Bemis said. "But you need to understand how things work in Washington. There is corrupt, and then there is…well, there are some people who just can't be touched."

Douglas frowned. "You brought me here to do a job. I'm doing that job. You said there'd be no interference."

Bemis smiled thinly at Douglas. "You'll thank me later. You don't work for government right now, but you might want to throw your hat in the ring sometime in the future. Some of these names, if you were to go public with them, they would ruin that future."

"I don't care about that," Douglas said. "You said you wanted me to dig out corruption."

"I did, and you're doing that," Bemis reassured Douglas. "Several of these names will serve as very good examples to keep other people in line. Now you keep building cases on these people and when the time is right, we'll turn this list," he hesitated, "our updated list, over to the Justice Department. Then we will shine the light on corruption in Washington like it's never been shone before."

Bemis put the paper he had been marking on back in the folder and handed it back to Douglas. As he did so, a knock came at the door, and Bemis' secretary entered.

"Senator Bemis, you wanted me to tell you when Dr. Singleton arrived," she said. "He's waiting for you."

Bemis nodded. "Send him in." He looked at Douglas.

"Thank you for your hard work, Douglas, and tell your wife to come next time."

Georgetown, Maryland

"Hello, D.J. Hello, Ruth." Bobby's face showed in the screen in the Center for Concerned Studies office as they called him on Zoom. "How's government work?"

"Not so good today," Douglas said. "Just got out of a meeting to reveal corruption to the Powers That Be. Turns out the Powers That Be are the ones who are corrupt."

Bobby chuckled. "Aren't they all. So, are you wanting to talk to me, or to Harris? Honestly, I'm not sure where he is right now, but I can probably find him."

"No, really, we just had some information we needed to share with others in the network," Ruth said. "About this guy named Anais Singleton."

"Oh, yes," Bobby said. "The stories I could tell."

"Me first," Douglas said. "I just ran into him going into a leading senator's office. Don't know if this senator is in his pocket, but I wouldn't be surprised."

"It doesn't take much," Bobby said. "Let me share with you what I've learned." He shared on the screen a video of Anais Singleton talking with Ian Target.

"This is in the penthouse of The Broadgate Tower in London a month ago," Bobby said. "Note the Interpol officers coming into the scene. Now watch what happens."

There was no audio with the image, but Ruth and Douglas could see the expression on the face of the officer in charge. Two of the uniformed officers began to choke, and the one in front suddenly became slack faced. A moment later, an officer dropped his gun. Singleton continued talking to the woman in front, as if talking to a young child. Finally, the woman turned, with the other officer picking up the gun, and they all turned and walked out of the scene.

"What happened?" Ruth asked. "Where did they go?"

"They were there to arrest Ian Target," Bobby said. "As you can see, they changed their minds. According to the police records, he wasn't there.

"I've been in contact with a fellow who used to work with Singleton as a biochemist at MI-6. Apparently, the process he was working on is based on pheromones, which means he doesn't have to have a gas, injection or pill to influence his victim. That's the bad news.

"The good news is that because of how it's passed from Singleton to others, he's the only one who can share it, and he can only do it with a limited number of people, say a room of less than thirty people."

"So he couldn't influence an audience over TV or radio," Ruth said. "And he couldn't persuade an entire stadium, like at the Super Bowl."

"Right," Bobby said. "As far as how long his influence lasts, we don't know that yet. I suspect maybe he doesn't even know."

"Well, I don't know if he's already influenced Senator Bemis or not, but we have our share of bad here," Douglas said. "With Bemis in bed with Singleton, what is the call here?"

"You're in a singular position right now," Bobby said. "You have access to power that none of the rest of us do. I know it puts you in an awkward place, but still."

"Ruth, I think it's time you opened that envelope from Harris," Douglas said. "You know the one I told you didn't matter?"

Ruth smiled ruefully. "Already have. We're right where we're supposed to be." She looked at her husband. "Harris knew what he was doing."

The two looked at each other, wondering what the future held.

"*Who knows but that you have come for such a time as this?*" paraphased Ruth from Esther 4:14. "We all have our parts to play, Bobby. Until we hear otherwise from Harris, we'll hang in here. We'll be the Heretics' eyes and ears in the Capitol."

* * *

City Council Meeting
City of Los Angeles

The mayor of Los Angeles, Donald K. Jackson, banged his gavel for attention.

"The representative from District 4 has requested that we allow Pastor Richard Escobar of the West Hills Congregational Church to address the City Council on a proposal. Pastor Escobar, you have the floor."

"Thank you, your honor," Pastor Escobar said. "It's a pleasure and a privilege to be here. I take my position as pastor of the West Hills Congregational Church seriously. I am a shepherd to my congregation of 5,000 members in West Hollywood, but many of them are not aware that I come from very different beginnings. In fact, I started out in East Los Angeles as the leader of a gang called the Ronin. We thought we were bad, and in reality, we terrified a lot of people. There weren't a lot of positives that could be taken from that experience. And were it not for the influence of one man and a mission that existed at that time, today I'd probably either be in prison or dead.

"My experience is not unique," he continued, walking around the floor in front of the fourteen city council members. "There are currently more than four hundred and fifty active gangs in the Los Angeles area with a membership of over forty-five thousand. If we can reach just a few of these young men and women, think of what that would mean for this community."

He paused and looked at the city council members, trying to gauge their reaction.

"Now I can't guarantee a positive response from every gang member," he said. "But in my day, the Children of God mission in East Los Angeles helped a lot of people, including me. It offered daycare, taught English classes, trained young people in practical skills like plumbing, electrical and drywall. And I even led out in a ministry of getting old cars running so that people could have transportation to get to work! More importantly, it taught people that they were precious in the eyes of God. It changed lives."

Once again, he looked at the City Council members, waiting for questions or a reaction. Finally, one spoke:

"What, Pastor, are you asking from us?" a bored looking woman asked.

"You've all been given a prospectus," Pastor Escobar told her. "We've gotten this going on a small scale, but I believe it's time to think big. Carry this project across Los Angeles. Stop gang violence! Help local communities! Think about it!"

"Yes, thank you, Pastor Escobar," the mayor said, interrupting. "Let's allow the Council members to examine the proposal, discuss it behind closed doors and we'll get back to you. Thanks for your visit."

Pastor Escobar nodded, then turned and unbuttoned his suit coat as he walked down the aisle to the outside doors, where Josh met him, standing up from his seat in the back row.

"They'd already made up their minds before I started speaking," Pastor Escobar muttered. "This was a waste of time."

"Maybe," Josh said. "I've heard that the government has become infiltrated by a group called Veritas. They have their own agenda. This could be the tip of the iceberg, the beginning of a bigger battle."

"Well, we haven't been beaten yet," Pastor Escobar said, shaking his head.

* * *

South Chicago

"So really," Moss said. "A Black Jesus?"

"To tell the truth," Taupe said. "Jesus was a Jew. He probably didn't look anything like any of the pictures you see of Him today. But He's the Savior of ALL mankind. White, Asian, Hispanic, Black. He loves gays and straights. He loves trans and bis. He loves racists. He loves Communists. He loves drug addicts and drug dealers. He even loves you jerks."

"People always paint God in their own image," Three Peat said. "We think of God as Our Father. When we say that, sometimes we have a hard time thinking good thoughts about the man who was our earthly father. But it helps to think about God as being a good, loving Father who cares about you. Because He does."

"Even with all the crap I done?" Shogun said. "I can't imagine God letting me into heaven after all the drugs and the women and the terrible things I done." He paused and looked at the floor soberly. "I killed an old lady once. Just turned and shot her like she was a dog. How God going to forgive me for that?"

"The hard part is forgiving ourselves sometimes," Taupe replied. "The Bible says, 'All have sinned and come short of the glory of God.' That's everyone. You, me, the preacher, and the hooker down the street. We're all sinners. We all need to repent. We all need Jesus."

"The Black Jesus," Shogun said.

Three Peat grinned at him. "Sure, if you want. The Black Jesus. Now, how about we all kneel right here and ask for God's forgiveness."

* * *

Austin, Texas

Back in the 1830s and 1840s, the frontier around Austin was designated by the Colorado River. East and north of the river was frontier town, which eventually became the capital of the fledgling Republic of Texas. West and south of the river, where the bluffs rose signaling the beginning of Texas Hill Country, was designated Comanche land. It had been that way when the Mexicans were in charge, and when the Spanish tried to settle the land before them. It was the rare white man—and woman—who dared venture across the river.

Connie wasn't thinking about that when she walked, bo staff in hand, toward the old railroad trestle bridge that spanned the river just north of Leroy Island. It was late evening. She was caught up in the memories of when she had first come across this forbidden span, ignoring the "Pedestrians Not Allowed" and "Do Not Cross" signs at the north entrance to find a quiet place to watch the water flow beneath her feet. It had been that way in her rebellious days when she had first come to Austin, when she had gotten involved with the Mystics, when she had met Marita. They had quickly become fast friends, had taken classes together, learned magic together, and had worked together as servers at The Roadhouse on Sixth Street. Even now, even with all that had happened, Connie saw Marita as her best friend.

As she quickly, but carefully, crossed the rough timbers that made up the trestle bridge that meant so much to them, she saw a familiar figure halfway across the bridge. It was Marita, and her heart thudded in her chest. She quickened her pace, and as she approached, Marita looked up, and then smiled.

"Thanks for coming," Marita said. "I didn't know how else to contact you."

Connie hesitated, then stepped forward and hugged Marita. Marita didn't resist her.

"Where's your escort?" Connie asked, pulling away. "The one I saw at the cafeteria?"

"I was lucky," Marita said. "I slipped out when he wasn't looking. He'll probably catch up in a few minutes, so I don't have a lot of time."

"What's going on?" Connie asked. "How can I help?"

"I don't know if there is a way to help," Marita said. "They never stop watching me. You were right. You were so, so right. They aren't locking me in a dungeon like before. But even if they let me come to school, it's just as much of a prison as it was before."

"Can you call the cops?" Connie said. "Detective Shapiro knows your story. He'll listen to you."

"No," Marita said, and started to cry. "You would be shocked at how many friends in high places they have. I don't dare report them. What I need...I can't have."

"What do you need?" Connie said. "Listen, you're my sister. I love you. Tell me what you need."

"I need...I need to get out of here. Far from here," she sobbed. "I need to disappear. To somewhere where no one knows me. Start over."

"Wow," Connie said. She hugged Marita again, and saw a dark figure coming onto the bridge from the southern side. "We've got company."

"It's him," Marita said, an edge of panic in her voice. "I came here because I wanted to throw myself in the river rather than go back with those people."

"No," Connie said, and then she had an idea. "I want to have a quick prayer with you, and then I have a gift for you. One that I think, I hope, will help solve your problems."

Connie hugged Marita and prayed for her, asking God to take care of her friend, and show her the path that He had chosen for her. Then they opened their eyes. Connie held out something in her hand to Marita.

"What is it?"

"If I'm right, I think it's a diamond," Connie said.

"Where did you get it?" Marita asked.

"It was payment for getting shot," Connie said wryly. When Marita's eyes opened wide, she shook her head. "Don't ask any more than that." She closed Marita's hand around the small gem.

"Take it," she said quietly. "Find a pawn shop or a jewelry store. Maybe you can get a few hundred or a few thousand dollars for it. Whatever you get, it should be enough to get you a bus ticket and a new start somewhere."

Marita stared at the diamond for a brief second more, then hugged Connie again.

"Now go," Connie said, looking at the rapidly approaching man. "I'll slow him down."

Marita disappeared behind Connie, who turned to face the approaching man. She stood on one of the timbers, her legs spread, her bo staff held across her chest. She watched silently as he came closer, then he stopped about ten feet away. The man was about six feet tall and about 200 pounds. Without the bo staff, there was no way she could slow him down, much less stop him. Now she prayed that she could do enough to let Marita get away.

"Get out of my way," the man growled. He was dressed in jeans and a leather coat, unlike the smaller man who had been dressed in a suit when Marita was on campus.

"Where's your friend?" Connie asked.

"I'm not telling you again," the man said, and he started to reach into his coat. Connie instantly guessed that he was reaching for a gun. Instinctively, she took two giant steps forward, bouncing on the balls of her feet on each timber before landing in front of him. As she did, she swung the bo staff above her head, then around to strike him on the back of the knees.

The wooden staff made a cracking sound with the impact, and the man collapsed. At the same time, Connie staggered herself with the impact of the bo staff hitting him, something she was surprised had happened.

Unfortunately, he didn't stay down for long. He rolled onto his feet and as he rose, and Connie realized that he already had a pistol in his hand. She swung the bo staff again, aiming for his gun hand. It hit the forearm of the hand with the pistol. The arm flew up in the air, with the pistol firing at the same moment. The crack of the pistol startled Connie, but she realized that he was now armed, so she needed to do more than delay him.

She spun and swung the bo staff with all her might at the back of his head. This time he ducked, and the staff sailed through open air. The movement and the lack of impact took Connie off balance, and she fell over. She lay on her side and looked up at the man, who stood above her with the pistol in his hand. He turned the pistol and looked at it, and Connie realized that he was in pain. Her strike on his forearm may have broken it. In either case, he was having a hard time holding the gun in his hand.

Seeing that she was down on the ground, he decided that she wasn't going to fight him anymore. He put the pistol back in his holster and started to run past her and after Marita. When Connie saw this, she realized that she needed to do something else. She stretched the bo staff out between his feet, and it tripped him up, causing him to stumble.

Cursing her, he struggled to get to his feet. In the meantime, Connie got to hers first. While he was getting up, she ran forward and gave him a kick in the side. It wasn't enough to hurt him, but it was just enough for him to lose his balance and fall off the side of the trestle bridge and into the cold waters of the Colorado River below.

Connie looked back toward town. Marita had already disappeared into the evening gloom.

"*Vaya con Dios*," she whispered to her friend. "Go with God."

19

In the Shadows

Connie had exactly twenty-four hours to get her act together after Marita left, because the next night was the big "Science, Magic, or Faith" Conference. So much had happened in the past few weeks: a whirlwind trip to Budapest, being shot, losing Miracle, losing her best friend, and the craziness of having everyone in her life gone. Now she was expected to address hundreds of people about what she believed, arguing that faith in God was stronger than the magic that she knew Katie Dawkins would bring to the conference, or that it made more sense than science to a room full of academics, as she knew Patrick Jackson would do.

More than once she considered calling up Prof. Valencia and telling him that she couldn't go up on that stage. She thought of a dozen excuses: her father was sick again, she was sick, she had a change of heart. But when it came down to it, she realized that anything she did would prove the other two participants were right, that Faith really wasn't that strong. For more than anything, she would have to depend on Faith—on Belief—to get her through the night.

She really didn't care whether her arguments won the night in the eyes of the audience. All she cared about was making sure that she didn't embarrass God. And then she asked herself, was that even possible? She thought back to I Corinthians 4:10: "We are fools for Christ…." If Paul was thinking about making a fool of himself all the way back in the first century—the *Apostle Paul*—who was she to worry about being embarrassed?

And then she prayed for God to send his Holy Spirit and give her the right words to speak. She turned her phone off a few hours before the presentation and spent a lot of her time in prayer and in looking up scripture, even though she knew that Prof. Valencia wouldn't allow scripture to be used as proof in the presentation. Therefore, she was surprised when her phone buzzed right before she went on stage. It was Maddie, her sister. She started to answer it, then saw that Harris Borden was standing in the backstage area, waiting for her. She was torn between her phone and Harris. He smiled at her.

"That's all right," he said quietly. "Take the call. I'll wait."

She smiled back at him, so thankful that he had come. She was still looking at him when she answered her phone and heard her sister's panicked voice.

"He's gone," she said. "Daddy's gone."

Connie blinked, staring at Harris, who saw in her face that something was wrong.

"You idiot, I told you," Maddie hissed. "Your father is dead. He had another heart attack."

"I…I will come right away," Connie said quietly, choking back a sob.

"Don't bother," Maddie said harshly. "You're too late." The phone call went dead.

Connie stared at Harris and dropped her phone. She stepped forward and blankly looked at the man who she respected more than any other man, except for the man who had just died.

"My father," Connie said. "He just died." She choked on the last word. Tears came freely and Harris stepped forward and embraced her. Connie began to sob.

"What's wrong? What did I just hear?" Prof. Valencia said, stepping forward.

"Her father just died," Harris said quietly, still holding her.

"Oh, that's terrible," Prof. Valencia said. "I'm so sorry. Well, obviously you're excused from going on tonight. The others will go on. It will be 'Science or Magic.' Just no Faith."

Harris looked at Prof. Valencia. "Is it possible for me to go on in her place? I mean, considering the situation?"

Prof. Valencia shook his head slowly. "That wouldn't be fair to the others, now really. You're a pastor, aren't you?"

Harris shrugged and nodded.

Connie sighed, cleared her throat, and sniffed. "No, I'll go on," she said. "I need to do this."

"No, that's impossible," Prof. Valencia said, handing her a handkerchief.

"No, my father would want me to," she said, taking it and putting it to her eyes. "I just need a minute."

Ten minutes later, Harris Borden had disappeared to join the audience, and Connie was lined up with Patrick Jackson and Katie Dawkins to go onstage. Her heart thudded in her chest, and her mind was clouded. As crazy as her life had been an hour ago, it had just all come crashing down. But she owed it to her father, who believed in God and the power of faith, to do her best tonight.

Prof. Valencia introduced each of the three participants individually, and they came out to sit on stools on the stage to mild applause. The professor stood behind a small podium at the side with each of them holding a microphone for their responses. He started with an explanation of the rules. The professor would ask three questions for all of them, followed by a chance for the audience to ask questions.

"Our first question for tonight: Does God exist? Is there any evidence that He does?"

Patrick Jackson held up his hand and jumped into this answer first.

"There is absolutely no evidence that God exists, or that He has ever existed," he said. "And since evidence—facts—are the basic cornerstone of science, that's why I don't believe in God, any more than I believe in Santa Claus, the Easter Bunny, or the Loch Ness Monster."

Prof. Valencia pointed at Katie Dawkins, who hesitated, then spoke up, choosing her words carefully.

"I believe in Gaia, the mother earth, from which all power and life comes," she said. "And because we have power, because we have life, we have a god. And that god is Gaia."

Patrick Jackson raised his fingers hesitantly and Prof. Valencia pointed at him.

"Are we allowed to ask questions of the other presenters?" he asked. Prof. Valencia nodded.

"Katie, you are saying that 'all power and life' comes from Gaia. Is that right?" he asked. She nodded. "What about the rest of the universe? The stars? What about solar energy? Does that come from Gaia too?"

"Well, of course not," she said, hesitantly.

"What about life on other planets?" Patrick asked. "Will Gaia allow life to exist on other planets?"

Prof. Valencia stepped in. "I don't intend for this to become a debate, but merely a comparison of perspectives. Patrick, I think you have made your point. Constance, do you have anything to add?"

Connie sat quietly and cleared her throat, her head pounding, and her lips dry as she looked out at the audience. At first, she looked in the first front rows to see if she could find Adam and Crash, but was disappointed when didn't see them, then looked toward the back. All she could see was a sea of strange faces. As she stared at them, she finally saw that Harris had taken a seat on the right side, near the back. Then she scanned across the same aisle to the opposite side on the left. There, seated on the far left aisle, was the arch witch who had imprisoned her several months before. Selah White.

She stared at her for a long minute in silence, with Selah White looking back at her and smiling faintly. The hackles rose on Connie's neck.

"Miss Simesçu, do you have something to add?" Prof. Valencia asked.

She cleared her throat again and finally spoke.

"The question is: Does God exist and do we have evidence of that. I look around me every day and see countless examples of evidence of God. Miracles of nature. Wonders that mankind has made because God has given us the knowledge, the skills to step forward and do them. But it is not evidence if you don't believe it's evidence. If I don't believe God exists, I can't believe He created nature. Therefore, I can't recognize the evidence that's right in front of my eyes. God gives us evidence. But we refuse to accept it because we refuse to accept Him."

She looked at Patrick, who started to open his mouth to speak, then decided not to.

"Question number two," Prof. Valencia asked. "Why do we exist? What is our purpose in the world?" He paused, then pointed at Patrick.

"We exist as a part of a natural cause and effect of evolution," Patrick said. "Starting with the Big Bang, then progressing through billions of years of evolution, we are the final product of that development on earth. Our purpose in the world is the same purpose as any other life form: to exist, to procreate, and to multiply. We feel the need to dominate our environment and hopefully, in the not-too-distant future, we will be able to move into space and inhabit other planets as well."

Katie raised her hand, and Prof. Valencia pointed at her.

"But that doesn't really give a reason why we exist," she said. "Do we have a purpose or are we an accident? Are we part of a plan?"

Patrick smiled smugly and answered.

"If there is no God, which I am sure there isn't, then how can there be a plan? I don't believe in a plan for the universe, or a plan for humanity. When we are born, our only goal in life is to live and survive. Maybe contribute something to humanity while we're alive. And when we die, the world will forget us and move on. That's how it's supposed to be."

"Sounds terrible," Katie said.

"What is your perspective on this, Katie?" Prof. Valencia asked. Patrick grinned and looked at her in expectation.

Katie closed her eyes and waved her hands in front of her. As the crowd gasped, sparks began to fly from her fingertips like fireflies. Despite the auditorium being properly lit, the lights began to dim, and people looked around them in amazement.

"We are but part of a whole," Katie began. "When we are born, we are an extension of Gaia. The more we understand and accept this, the more we will be at peace with the universe. Magic is simply Gaia's will as it is expressed through us when we allow her to speak. Our purpose is to do Gaia's will."

She stopped the waving of her hands, and the lights brightened again, with the sparks disappearing. There was a hush, then people began applauding.

"How'd you do that?" Patrick hissed, frowning.

"Very well. Constance?" Prof. Valencia asked, pointing her direction. Hearing her name made her realize that the fog had returned, and Connie hadn't really been listening to what the others had been saying.

"What was the question again?" she asked.

"The question is: why do we exist? What is our purpose in the world?"

Connie hesitated, then thought about everything that had happened in the past few months. It somehow was all starting to make some sense.

"As a Christian, we are taught that our purpose is to show the world what God is like by being as much like him as we can," Connie said. "I know that a lot of my fellow Christians don't act much like Christ. And that's a problem. Maybe it's because we make it too difficult to understand. And I think the mission is one that you don't have to be a Christian to do. You don't even have to be a believer."

"And what is that, Constance?" Prof. Valencia asked.

"What would this world be like if we were all just a little kinder to each other?" she asked. The auditorium was quiet for a long moment, then there were hoots of derision from several in the audience.

"Now, I know that some of you think that's a simplistic view of the world," she said. "It's an opportunity for others to take advantage of you. Well, maybe that's the problem. Maybe we're so concerned of others taking advantage of us that we look for every opportunity to take advantage of everyone else. What if we thought about others before ourselves for once?"

A few applauded, but most of the college-aged listeners hooted and booed.

* * *

Petronus Twin Towers
Kuala Lumpur, Malaysia

"It's quite unusual for the Consortium to gather again when it hasn't been a year yet," Anais Singleton said to the gathered members of the billionaires' club. "Think of it as an excuse for all of us to enjoy the spectacular view from here."

He gestured behind him through the glass wall at the night vista behind him showing Kuala Lumpur. The others had seen it before, that much was sure, but at this point, no one was going to argue with him.

Singleton shrugged. "Or you can say I just missed you fellows. Living on the road gets quite lonely, and as popular as I have become in recent days, I still don't have many people I can consider true and faithful friends. Not like you lot."

He smiled and the men around the table smiled back at him.

"Now, on to business," he said. "Phase One is basically complete. I've met with government and law enforcement leaders in select locations and made them realize that they needed to fall in line. That part took time but was necessary. I use the word 'basically,' because as powerful as my influence is, it's not foolproof. Apparently, some of you still insist on doing things your own way."

He paused and looked at the group as if instructing a class of second graders.

"I have access to funds from all of your banks," Singleton said. "And I truly appreciate your cooperation. All but one." He turned and looked at the man sitting on the corner of the table.

"Mr. Estevez," Singleton said. "Why haven't you provided me access to your offshore accounts? Don't you trust me?"

Sergio Estevez forced a smile onto his lips and looked up into Singleton's face.

"You have access to close to a trillion dollars right now. Why do you need my accounts?"

Singleton smiled. "Sergio, you're missing the point. This is a club. We do everything *together*. Get it? *Together*."

Estevez stared at Singleton. "You're not in control of me. I know your mind games. You won't control me."

Singleton sighed. "I hate that it has to be this way." He turned to the others.

"Sergio doesn't want to play along. Why don't you four take him out onto the balcony. Make him see his mistake. If he won't change his mind, throw him off."

Four of the billionaires rose from their seats and grabbed Sergio Estevez and began to drag him out the door of the small dining room.

"Wait, wait," Estevez said. "Okay, I'll sign." They let him go, and he smoothed his suit and hair. One of them brought a laptop over to him and he pressed his thumb up to the digital identifier, then typed in a line on the page.

"There," he said, staring at Singleton. "It's all yours. Satisfied?"

"Not really," Singleton said. "We can't have bad apples in our club. Boys, go ahead and take him outside."

Estevez began to scream and struggle, but the four men grabbed him and dragged him out the door while the others watched. From where they were, the rest of them could see Estevez struggling against the other four men.

"So apparently your influence isn't one hundred percent effective," Ian Target said quietly to Singleton.

Singleton chuckled. "It will be in a minute." There was a scream as Estevez was thrown off the balcony and to his death a thousand feet below. "You see, if you have enough believers on your side, one person who disagrees isn't a problem."

Ian Target shook his head. "You realize that you could be master of the world with such a gift!" He beamed at Singleton. "Emperor for life!"

The other men shouted their agreement.

"Remember when I first came to you men?" Singleton said. "You thought that money was the key to unlimited power. I showed you the error of your ways. You're still making those mistakes."

The men looked at each other, confused.

"Gentlemen, we're going to change the world, that is true. But I have no plans to become an emperor of the world. For I know that an emperor is always likely to be assassinated by those who don't understand what he's trying to do."

He paused and looked at the men, as if he were looking for the right words.

"We are entering Phase II, a critical phase in my plan to save this world. And for this to work, I will need to disappear. I'll work best when I work from the shadows. The world won't see me, but I'll still be there. Influencing. Controlling. And in some cases, eliminating obstacles."

He smiled at the men in front of him and nodded.

"In the next few years, you may not see me, but you'll see my effect. For I'm still in control." He smiled and winked. "Goodbye, gentlemen." 𝒱

20

Exodus

"And for my third and final question," Prof. Valencia said into the microphone, looking at the three participants on stage. "Is there such a thing as good and evil in the world?"

The dull rustle of whispering came to a complete silence in the large auditorium as the professor signaled for Katie Dawkins to answer the question.

Katie responded by inhaling slowly through her nose, then nodding. She took her hands and slowly began rolling an invisible ball between them as she spoke.

"Some people look at magic as a good thing; others think of it as evil. I know for a fact that it is neither good nor evil. It is simply a tool to be used by those in power. There are white witches who do good things in the world, such as the mission we have here in town where we help people in need. And there are other witches who practice black magic. They are intent on power alone, regardless of who it hurts."

The area within her hands began to light up, and as she spoke, a ball of fire appeared in the center of it. The crowd began to gasp and watched closely.

"Evil is hurting someone so that you can get ahead," Katie said, continuing. "There is too much of that in the world. And I am very much opposed to it."

She held her hand open for the audience to see, and the ball of flame glowed there briefly before disappearing with a whoosh. The audience oohed and then burst into applause.

"Not sure they heard any of what she said," muttered Patrick loud enough that Connie could hear. She was watching the rear of the auditorium, where Selah White was sitting. Her eyes were closed, but

Connie knew she wasn't sleeping. She was somehow helping Katie with her magic.

"Patrick, how do you respond to the question?" Prof. Valencia asked, pointing at him.

Patrick raised his microphone to his mouth.

"From a strictly scientific perspective, I can't believe in good and evil any more than I can believe in the supernatural," Patrick said. "The natural world is simply a world of survival, of cause and effect, of action and reaction. There are no good guys and bad guys. As they say, history is written by the victors. Those who win are the good guys and those who lose are evil.

"That being said, I've seen evil in my own life. I had a brother who was gunned down by a drive-by while he was walking home from school. He'd done nothing wrong; he had no enemies. And yet, someone decided that he should die that day."

Connie looked at Patrick, and suddenly saw his cynical, hardened shell crack and realized he was hurting inside. Beneath the snide remarks and the callous name calling was a young man who had lost someone he loved. And with it, he realized that there was more to life than science.

"I may not believe in God, but I do know that evil exists."

* * *

South Chicago

It was a historic meeting, one that was not without controversy. Four of the biggest gangs in Chicago had agreed to unite, not to sell drugs, to destroy another gang, or promote prostitution, but to help their community. It was controversial because not everyone in their gangs agreed with the treaty, and in fact, many were thinking that it was some sort of hoax. But the leaders of the four gangs—the Lords, the Disciples, the Cobras, and the Hustlers—had met several times and had decided not only to lay down their guns but to cooperate to make South Chicago a better place for people to live.

"Look at this," Taupe said, smiling and talking to Three Peat, the big man and tall Black woman standing and leaning on the pool house outside the luxurious home of Shogun, where they were meeting. "You should be very proud of yourself."

"I am," Three Peat said, staring at more than fifty gang members who continued to file into the backyard and take their seats on the folding chairs set up there. "But I'm not fool enough to believe I could have done this without your help."

"God's help," Taupe corrected him. "I just went where He directed me. Did what He asked me to. That's what it always comes down to."

"So this new job of yours, the one that you've been so cryptic about?" Three Peat asked. "It wouldn't have anything to do with what you did here, would it?"

Taupe laughed. "Guilty. Not every job is like this. And I'll have to admit I was scared to come back to my home turf. But God knew what he was doing."

"Well, I'm glad you came," Three Peat said. "Come on. They're about to sign the treaty. You won't want to miss this." He started walking toward the small platform they had set up in front of the chairs.

"Just a second," Taupe said. "Let me grab my phone." She turned and ducked into the pool house to grab her iPhone. A moment later, she was coming out when she noticed uniformed men coming through the gate and over the fence, armed with automatic weapons.

"Everyone down! This is the police!" she heard them shout.

A moment later, she saw at least two gang members jump up and pull pistols out and begin to shoot. A second after that, the air was filled with bullets.

"Taupe!" she heard Three Peat shout as he ran in her direction, just before she saw bullets pepper his chest, and he fell. Several others dropped to the ground, and she saw still others hold up their hands in surrender, but the bullets kept flying. She suddenly realized that the two gang members who had pulled weapons had been shot down immediately, but all the shooting after that was from the uniformed police. And then she noticed something else.

The back of the Kevlar-vested uniforms said POLICE, but on the shoulder of each officer was a stylized **Ɣ**. Taupe remembered the message she had gotten from Ruth about Veritas, and immediately made the connection. Even now, as she realized the gang members were no longer putting up resistance, the officers were continuing to shoot everyone in sight.

Taupe crawled back to the pool room and opened her cell phone. She dialed a number that she had hoped she would never have to dial. Twice before she had sent out the dreaded "helter skelter" signal to evacuate. But this time was different. This time, she was afraid she wouldn't survive to get the message out.

She dialed the number, and it rang twice before going to voice mail.

"Harris," she hissed. "Veritas is here. They are dressed like cops. And they are killing everyone in sight. Pray for me. Pray for us all."

A second later, the door exploded open, and a uniformed officer sprayed the inside of the pool room with automatic gunfire.

* * *

Harris Borden was watching Connie on the stage, proud of her responses, and praying for her considering her circumstances. He noticed that she kept looking at a woman with long, white hair who sat in the back opposite him, and he realized that the woman was probably the one they called Selah White, the witch. He looked at the woman, and tried to get a measure of her, but couldn't. Often he could sense evil in certain people, but with her, he could only sense a vast barrier as if something were protecting her. Once, she looked at him while he was looking at her. She raised an eyebrow and smiled, then quickly looked away.

That's someone to keep an eye on, he thought to himself. And then his phone buzzed. It was the middle of the presentation, and he didn't want to miss any of it, but he looked at the number and realized that it was from Taupe. She never called unless it was important. He sat for a moment, indecisive. A voice mail appeared on the screen. Harris decided to get up and go out to the lobby to hear what it said.

* * *

West Hills Congregational Church
West Hollywood

"Do you all realize how precious you are to me?" Pastor Escobar said to the congregation during that Wednesday night meeting. The response was a murmur of approval, followed by applause. "Tonight officially marks six years since you so graciously took me in as shepherd for this congregation. And look how God has blessed us!" He turned and looked around him. "Think about it! Think about yourselves and how God has blessed each of you in turn in the past six years! God is good, isn't He?"

The congregation burst into applause again, and Pastor Escobar applauded with them.

"Most of you have no clue where I come from, and yet you have accepted me as one of your own," Pastor Escobar continued. "So I decided that tonight was the night that I share that information with you."

An image popped up on the two gigantic screens above his head. It showed two young Hispanic boys, about age eight and nine, arm in arm, outside a broken-down barrio in East Los Angeles. They were grinning, and the taller one had a black eye.

"This is me with my brother, Julio," Pastor Escobar said. "He was one year older than me. We grew up on the streets in East Los Angeles. Julio joined a gang when he was fourteen, and I joined the same gang a year later. Julio died in a shootout with police when he was sixteen. I was luckier than most."

The screen above him switched to him as a young man, barely twenty, dressed in leathers, tattoos up and down his arms, smoking a cigarette, leaning against a motorcycle. Others who looked like him stood around him.

"When our leader was arrested and our gang was disbanded, a few of my friends and I started the gang known as the Ronin. We terrorized East Los Angeles for close to ten years. That is, until a pastor named Harris Bordon arrived. At first, I didn't believe he was for real, talking about his Master and how he would give me direction, a focus for my life. But he was telling the truth. Pastor Borden—we knew him as Elijah Brown—changed my life and the lives of many others in that neighborhood."

The image on the screen switched to a modern-day photo of the Mission, the way they had found it: boarded up, dusty, with weeds in every crack in the pavement.

"This building is the Mission for the old Children of God. They used to be everywhere, with the sole purpose of helping people like me get on their feet, find a purpose in life, and sometimes find God, or as in my case, learn to help other people. I hadn't been back there for several years. A friend of mine was sent here to remind me of my roots. He was sent here to remind me that we can't really call ourselves Christians if we don't go out of our way to help other people. This is your opportunity to prove that you deserve that name."

He turned and gestured off the stage, where Josh was waiting.

"Ladies and gentlemen, brothers and sisters, this is Joshua Brown. Please listen to him."

As Josh stepped forward and began his appeal to the congregation to help resurrect the Mission, Pastor Escobar stepped off the stage and entered the hallway behind the stage where his old office was located. His intent was to change the battery on his lapel microphone, which he knew was almost dead. But as he entered the hallway, he realized that someone was in his old office, the room with the sign that read: Private.

The door was slightly ajar, and he pulled it open to look in. It was one of the deacons, kneeling on the floor of the office, crying.

"Thomas, you startled me," Pastor Escobar said. "Is there something I can help you with?"

The young deacon stood up suddenly. He reached up with his left hand and put it on the pastor's shoulder, and his right hand held a long-bladed stiletto knife, which he jabbed into the pastor's upper stomach, making sure to shove it up and through the diaphragm. Pastor Escobar's eyes grew wide, and he looked at the deacon in shock.

"I'm sorry," the deacon said, tears still in his eyes. "Please forgive me."

* * *

"Now it's time for questions from the audience," Prof. Valencia said. "But before we do, let's agree on some guidelines. First, tonight is provided so that we can share a variety of perspectives. It's not a debate. There are no wrong and right answers. Second, please refrain from profanity and insults. Third, please try to focus on the subject matter here at hand. I encourage you to remember that these participants are students just like you. Please treat them with the respect that you would want if you were up here."

A dozen hands went up in the audience, and the professor pointed at the first one. It turned out being a hard science question having to do with the age of the universe, which he turned over to Patrick. Patrick answered it quickly.

The second question came from a Robert Fua, a junior business major, sitting three rows from the front.

"This question is for Connie," he said. "How do you justify serving a God that allows all the terrible things to happen in the world? If he loved us, why doesn't he just get rid of all the death and disease and wars and terrible storms?"

Connie smiled at the answer, then paused.

"That question is one that has been raised for a very long time," she answered. "In fact, it's one of the arguments that Satan, the leader of everything that is evil, has presented to the rest of the world and to the universe. If God is so good, why does he let bad things happen?"

She paused, thinking of her father, and the words caught in her throat.

"It's because we live in a world where we have choice," she said. "And a long time ago, our parents chose to leave God and live independent of Him. But what they didn't understand is that we are in a war where there is no middle ground. If you're not on God's side, then Satan has you. And when you follow Satan, terrible things happen."

She paused again, the words struggling to come out.

"I lost someone very special to me tonight," she said. "My father died right before we came out here. And it wasn't because he didn't love God. It wasn't because God was punishing us, or because God is mean or cruel. It is because we live in this terrible world."

By this time, the tears were streaming down her face, but she kept speaking, the words coming out in halting tones.

"And I for one am looking forward to leaving it one day, so that I can be with my father again!"

Several people began to applaud, but just as many began to boo.

* * *

Josh finished the last words of his prepared speech and thanked the congregation. They responded with a polite applause. He was surprised by the hundreds who had come out for a Wednesday night meeting, which he realized was more due to the charisma of Pastor Escobar than anything he could say. Josh knew that he wasn't much of a public speaker, and he was surprised when Pastor Escobar insisted that Josh be the person that made the appeal for support of the new Mission.

As it was, he caught the eye of several businessmen as he was exiting the stage, who gave him a thumbs up, indicating that they were on board to support the project. That gave him a feeling of hope.

Maybe Harris really did know what he was doing when he sent him here.

As he left the platform and headed for the hallway where the pastor had gone, his phone began to buzz silently. He pulled it out and looked at it and realized it was Harris.

"Good news, boss," Josh said. "Apparently the Mission project is a go."

As he spoke, he walked down the darkened hallway toward Pastor Escobar's old office. He realized that the doorway was standing open, and as he got closer, he saw that feet were sticking out of the doorway, extending into the hall.

"Never mind the Mission," Harris was saying on the phone. "Taupe's been shot."

Josh had already pulled his phone from his ear when he saw Pastor Escobar's body lying on the carpeted floor. He felt for a pulse but didn't feel one.

"Somebody call 911!" he shouted out the door. A moment later, a deacon, then another, came running into the room. The second one ran out to get help.

"He doesn't have a pulse," Josh said. "Lost too much blood." He looked down and realized that there was blood puddled on the carpet, on his suitcoat, and on his hands. Then he realized that Harris was still on the phone, waiting for him.

Several other people rushed into the hallway, followed by two with a stretcher.

"Back up, please," they said. "We're medical personnel."

Josh stood up and backed up, then continued to back up and out the door. Finally, he was outside the hallway in the alley.

"Harris? Are you still there?" Josh said, remembering that he was still holding the phone.

"Yes, I'm still here," Harris said. "Did you hear me?"

"Something about Taupe getting shot?"

"She called and left a message that Veritas had invaded the meeting she was in, disguised as police, and started shooting everyone. I think they'll be after everybody."

"Helter skelter?" Josh asked.

"Not exactly," Harris said. "But you need to leave now. I want you in Seattle."

"Home turf, huh?" Josh said. "Not sure how I feel about that."

"Well, if Taupe can do it, so can you. But disappear. Now."

"Got it," Josh said.

Josh took one more look at the young pastor lying on the carpeted floor of the large church in West Hollywood, then he took off the blood-stained suitcoat he was wearing and dropped it in the nearest trashcan.

Forty-five minutes later, he was on a bus to Seattle.

21

Egress

Bates Recital Hall
University of Texas
Austin, Texas

One minute Harris Borden was standing in an empty lobby of a recital hall, talking on his cell phone. He had just hung up from speaking with Josh and was dialing Ruth's number to warn her of everything that had happened. That was when the universe turned upside down.

The lights around him went black. He felt the floor collapse and he felt like he was falling, falling, as if he were in an elevator shaft. His heart caught in his throat. And then came a smothering feeling of closeness, a suffocating feeling like heavy blanket after heavy blanket were being thrown over him. He was being smothered, and at the same time he was falling forever.

A voice laughed, a woman's voice.

"Do you feel that, Mr. Borden?" the voice said. "That is the feeling you get when you have been outclassed. You're dealing way out of your league here, now, pastor. I'm Selah White, a grand witch, one of the most powerful on earth. And now there is nothing you can do but surrender to the inevitability of your fate. For this is what *hell* feels like!"

The feeling of falling increased and the stifling, suffocating feeling filled his lungs. But Harris didn't panic. Instead, he looked up in the direction where the voice had come from and shook his head.

"Apparently you didn't get the memo. You haven't a clue whom you're dealing with."

The woman's voice cackled in laughter.

"Oh, yes, I've heard of your exploits, as overblown as I think they are," she said. "I'm not worried about you."

It was then Harris' turn to chuckle.

"What's so funny?" Selah White asked.

"You don't get it," Harris said. "I'm not talking about me. I'm talking about Him."

Harris pointed up, and then knelt and began praying. Suddenly the falling motion stopped, and the suffocating feeling began to dissipate. A moment after that, cracks of light appeared above his head, and then the entire dark universe crumbled and exploded.

A brilliant white light poured from the sky and covered Harris Borden, who remained on his knees. Instead of a laughing witch, Harris began to hear a shrieking.

"The light! Stop it! It's blinding me!"

* * *

Connie and the two other presenters were standing on the floor below the stage, answering questions and thanking people for coming when a young male student crashed through the doors.

"Something's happened," he said. "Call 911."

The audience began to surge through the doors, and Connie looked around to see what might have happened. She realized that with hundreds of students in front of her, she wouldn't be getting out to the lobby anytime soon. And then she realized that Harris Borden was nowhere around.

She saw Prof. Valencia ahead of her, standing in the aisle, and waved at him.

"Do you know what happened?" she asked, the crowd surging past her. By this time, she began to hear sirens. Valencia shook his head.

"I heard someone say that there was some sort of attack," he said. "One of our former professors, Dr. Selah White, appears to be blinded."

"Blinded? How did it happen?" she asked, while the two of them still struggled to get to the lobby. Prof. Valencia shook his head.

Finally, they got through to the lobby, and found that the police had arrived. They had cordoned off one section of the lobby and were directing the audience to leave through the side doors. Connie and Prof. Valencia pushed as close as they could to the line of police officers. On the other side, Connie saw Selah White on a gurney being wheeled out of the lobby area and toward a waiting ambulance. Bandages covered the top half of her face.

Across from her, two uniformed officers were handcuffing Harris Borden. He looked up and locked eyes with Connie, who wanted to say something—anything—to this man who was a second father to her, especially on this day when she needed him so much. But he shook his head slightly. *No*, he was telling her. Then she noticed the stylized **𝒱** on the shoulder of each of the uniformed officers. *Veritas.*

"Isn't that the man who was with you backstage?" Prof. Valencia asked. "What happened?"

"I have no idea," Connie said, still staring as they walked Harris toward a waiting police car.

Get out of here, she heard a voice say to her. *Run.*

"This is probably not the right time to say it," she heard behind her. She turned and saw Patrick Jackson talking to her, his tie pulled askew. Katie Dawkins stood behind him. "But I thought you did a wonderful job up there. I just found out about your father. I'm so sorry for your loss." He held out his hand for her to shake.

"Thank you, Patrick," she said, taking his hand. She looked at Prof. Valencia, who smiled.

"Yes, you all did great," the professor said. "I'd like to take you three to dinner to celebrate."

Run, she heard again.

"Sorry to be a party pooper," Connie said. "But I have a prior commitment. I'll see you guys in class."

Run? She thought. *Where would I run?* The thought made no sense to her. All that she knew is that she was drained with everything that had happened. She still hadn't had a chance to absorb the news of her father's death, and on top of that, Harris was now in the hands of Veritas. All she could think to do was go and be with Adam.

Fortunate for her, there were students headed back to the dorms and she caught a ride from one of the cars lined up outside the performance hall. The two girls she rode with babbled about the presentation, but her mind was clouded with everything that was going on. It was all she could do to nod and smile at their compliments. A few minutes later, she was on Guadalupe Street, dropped off in front of Reborn Books.

It was late, but she hoped that Adam was still up. Thankfully, as she neared the bookstore, she saw that the lights were still on. The front door was locked, but she figured Adam was either on his computer going through inventory or paying bills. She rapped on the glass door, and a minute later, Adam appeared at the door.

He was wearing a hoodie and sweatpants and looked like he had been asleep.

"Well, it's late but I'm glad you came," Adam said, opening the door.

"Adam, I'm so glad to see you," Connie said. She rushed forward and hugged his neck, tears falling freely. Adam hesitated, surprised, then reacted by hugging Connie back.

"Everything okay?" Adam asked.

"No, everything is not okay," she said. "Dad died tonight."

"Oh, baby, I'm sorry," he said. "Come on inside. I'll put some coffee on."

"Not only that, but Harris has been arrested."

"Arrested?"

"Taken. By Veritas."

"Oh my—," he said. "Wow. That makes the news I have a lot less important."

"What news is that?"

"Maybe it'll help a little," Adam said. He handed her a box of tissues. "Miracle came back. He's upstairs. Why don't you go up and see him and I'll get coffee? And then we can talk all night if you want."

"Sounds great," Connie said, still sniffing. "Let me go see my precious puppy."

She took the box of tissues with her and climbed the stairs to the apartment. She opened the door and poked her head inside.

"Miracle?" she called. When there was no answer, she stepped inside. There was no dog inside, and it appeared as if nothing had changed from the last time she was there. She wandered around the small apartment, but saw no trace that Miracle was there.

"Well, a hundred-pound dog couldn't hide that well," she muttered. She turned to go back out the door and down the stairs. She saw that her denim jacket with the sequined "Eat at Joe's" message on the back—the one that had already saved her life once—was hanging on the back of a chair there. Smiling, she put it on over her formal dress.

"Now I feel more like myself," she said. She opened the door and started to go down the stairs, only to see Adam standing below her.

"Is the coffee on?" Connie asked.

"Not quite," Adam said. He raised an automatic pistol and aimed it at her.

"Adam, what are you doing?" Connie said.

"Something I don't want to do," he said. "But it's what Dr. Singleton wants. It's what Veritas wants. I'm so sorry." He pulled the hammer back on the pistol. "Connie, I love you."

Connie turned and threw her left arm up just as Adam fired. The bullet grazed the denim jacket that Connie was wearing and deflected off, embedding in the wall behind her. But the force of the bullet was enough to throw her backward into the room.

This time, she wasn't knocked unconscious. She felt the sting of the bullet as it slammed her arm and shoulder, but it hit at an angle, so she didn't get the full force of it. Even so, she felt her arm go numb.

"Connie?" she heard Adam say below her. "Connie, are you all right? Please say you're all right."

"Oww," Connie groaned, and she stood and slammed the door between her and Adam. "No, I'm *not* all right!" she shouted back at him. She turned the new deadbolt that Adam had added after the recent break-in.

She heard him climb the steps and rattle the doorknob.

"Connie, please let me in. I need to explain," he said. "I promise I won't hurt you."

'Yeah, like that's going to happen," she said. "You shot me. Go away!"

"I'm sorry for what happened. I'm sorry about the gun. That's all done. Veritas doesn't have any control over me now."

Connie bit her lip and began to cry again.

"Adam, I wish I could believe you," Connie said. "I need to believe you. Who else do I have in this world?"

There was a long pause, and Connie pulled out her cell phone, wondering if she should call the police. But if they were all Veritas, like they were at the performance, what then? Then she remembered that she had the number for Detective Shapiro.

She dialed it and she heard his voice mail. She left a message.

"Detective Shapiro," she said quickly. "This is Connie Simesçu. My ex-boyfriend, Adam Target is shooting at me with a pistol. Please come and help me. We're at the Reborn Bookstore on Guadalupe. Please hurry."

When she hung up, she realized that she smelled smoke. She put her hand to the door and it felt warm. Then white smoke started to creep under the doorway.

"Adam, what are you doing?" she shouted. "You're going to burn your bookstore down!"

"See what you're making me do?" Adam said. "This bookstore has already been through one fire. What's another fire to reclaim the woman I love?"

"You are absolutely crazy," Connie said. "And you're not reclaiming me. You're trying to kill me."

"If you're going to spend the night splitting hairs, we'll never get anywhere."

"Adam, please put out the fire," Connie said, trying to sound as rational as possible.

"Do you promise to forgive me?" Adam asked.

"Yes, I'll forgive you," Connie said, coughing. The smoke was now filling the room she was in. She grabbed a T-shirt that lay nearby and soaked it in the sink. Then she put it over her nose and mouth.

"Unlock the door and come down," Adam said.

"Adam, put out the fire!" she shouted. Connie saw the door glowing orange, and suddenly realized that she would not be able to get out that door, even if she wanted to. She was trapped.

Suddenly she heard a crash behind her. She turned and saw glass on the floor from the skylight. She walked over to it and looked up into a familiar face.

"Hello there," Crash said. "Would you like some help?"

Connie nodded. "Sure, but I don't think you're strong enough to lift me the ten feet to the roof. And I think I broke my arm."

Crash grinned. "That's why I brought help."

A thick nylon rope with a harness fell to the floor in front of her. A second later, Stevie's face joined Crash's in the skylight above Connie.

"Strap in," Stevie said. "We'll have you out of there in no time."

Even with her formal dress and a broken arm, it didn't take Connie more than a minute to get the harness on her. A minute after that, they were on the roof together. Connie immediately realized that the air outside was a lot fresher than the air in the smoky room.

"Well," she said. "I'm not really dressed for jumping across rooftops." She smiled at her two rescuers. "But thanks for coming."

"I've done you one better," Crash said. "I've been watching the way things are going. Stevie and I think it's time you run. Too many people you care about are getting hurt. We don't want you hurt too."

"Run?" Connie echoed. "That's not the first time I've heard that tonight. But run where? Where can I disappear to? I don't even have a change of clothes."

Stevie reached behind him and dropped a duffel bag in front of Connie.

"I got a chance to meet your roommate Dorie," Stevie said. "Said you were leaving on a long trip, and that you needed her to pack for you. Sweet girl."

Connie stared at them, then shook her head, still confused.

"Look, between me and Stevie, we can keep you safe here on the streets," Crash said. "Trust us."

"Yeah, you already did so much for us," Stevie growled. "Let us do this for you."

* * *

When Detective Shapiro arrived at Reborn Bookstore, it was already fully engulfed in flames. Firefighters had arrived and were focused on keeping the fire from spreading to the shops on either side of the bookstore. Two black-and-white patrol cars were there as well, mostly to keep the curious back. Shapiro noticed that one was standing by Adam Target, who sat on the back entrance of an ambulance, receiving oxygen.

Shapiro stepped up to the police officer who stood by Adam and asked him, "Has he said anything?"

The officer nodded. "He confessed everything. Shot at his girlfriend. Set the fire."

Adam pulled the oxygen away. "It wasn't my fault," he said. "I was told to."

"Okay," Shapiro asked. "And who was it that told you to shoot Connie?"

"Anais Singleton," Adam said. "He's to blame."

Shapiro nodded, then shrugged. "That's that billionaire in the news. It will make for an interesting court case." He turned and looked at the inferno in front of him. Then he walked over to the fire chief a few steps away.

"I believe there is still a young woman inside," Shapiro said. "Any chance of her surviving this?"

The fire chief shook his head. "It was fully engaged when we got here. If there was a woman inside, she's gone now."

"How long before we can check for a body?"

"As hot as that fire is?" the fire chief said. "It will be several days at least."

Shapiro stared at the fire. No, he wasn't willing to give up on Connie Simescu quite yet. He had seen her survive too much already.

One little fire wouldn't be enough to do her in. **γ**

Epilogue

Dallas, Texas

Mathias Simesçu had a lot more friends that he realized. The funeral at the small church they attended was full to overflowing, with flowers and well-wishes coming from hundreds of people. Over the years, he had had a positive influence on many people in his church, in his neighborhood, and in his community. Alina, his wife, was overwhelmed by the many people who called, sent messages, or left food and other gifts at her door. It was exhausting. Had it not been for her daughter Madelyn Simms, who cancelled a trip to be with her mother, the whole experience would have been a lot more difficult.

The graveside service was more of a relief. After the pandemonium of the large funeral, Alina had insisted on family only at the graveside. And so it was that Maddie and her mother were alone by the grave with the minister and the body of Mathias Simesçu for one last opportunity to say goodbye.

After the pastor had said what he intended, and the casket was gradually being lowered into the ground, Maddie and Alina stood silently by the graveside. At last, they were alone.

"I'm sorry that Connie wasn't here," Maddie said.

"I am not," Alina said. "Your father understood."

"What are you talking about?" Maddie asked.

"Constance told us that she was called by God," Alina said. "We accepted that. Mathias gave his blessing." She looked at Connie's older sister. "You need to accept it too."

Maddie said nothing but nodded slowly.

"I still miss her," Maddie said, putting her arm around her mother.

"So do I," Alina said, patting Maddie's arm. "So do I."

Maddie took in a deep breath and stepped away from her mother. She turned and looked around them. The cemetery workers were politely standing off at a distance, giving the two women their last few moments alone before they came in to cover the grave and Mathias' final resting place. Beyond them, hundreds of other graves spread out across the green lawn.

And on a hillside in the distance, Maddie saw a single figure standing, watching them. The stranger was wearing a black hoodie that covered his or her face, but they were not very big, and one arm was in a sling.

Beside the stranger stood a very large dog on a leash.

Maddie opened her mouth to say something, then stopped and smiled as the figure turned and walked away. *ᗯ*

END OF BOOK TWO

BIBLE VERSES USED
OR REFERRED TO IN THIS BOOK:

"Behold, I send you forth as sheep in the midst of wolves: be ye therefore wise as serpents, and harmless as doves." Matthew 10:16 (KJV)

"For our struggle is not against flesh and blood, but against the rulers, against the authorities, against the powers of this dark world and against the spiritual forces of evil in the heavenly realm." Ephesians 6:12 (NIV)

"You are the salt of the earth. But if the salt loses its saltiness, how can it be made salty again? It is no longer good for anything, except to be thrown out and trampled underfoot." Matthew 5:13 (NIV)

"Blessed are the poor in spirit, for theirs in the kingdom of heaven." Matthew 5:1 (NIV)

"Blessed are you when people insult you, persecute you and falsely say all kinds of evil against you because of me." Matthew 5:11 (NIV)

"We are fools for Christ, but you are so wise in Christ! We are weak, but you are so strong! You are honored, we are dishonored!" I Corinthians 4:10 (NIV)

"And who knows but that you have come to your royal position for such a time as this?" Esther 4:14b (NIV)

"For all have sinned and fall short of the glory of God." Romans 3:23 (NIV)

"Then Samuel said, 'Speak, for your servant is listening.'" I Samuel 3:10b NIV

If you enjoyed this book, you may also like other books by the author. They include:

Digital and Print:
Tom Horn vs. The Warlords of Krupp
The Kiss of Night
Infinity's Reach
If Tomorrow Comes
Not My Son, Lord
Write Thinking: Psychology for the Productive Writer
The Champion
The Heretic
Elijah
Chosen
Tesla's Ghost
The Key of Solomon (Foundation Series Book #2)
Soul Survivor (The Heretics Series Book #1)

Digital Only:
52 Things to Do on Sabbath
The Stranger and Other Stories
A Hole in the Sky and Other Stories
The Last Supper

Print Only:
The Shoebox Kids: The Mysterious Treasure Map
The Shoebox Kids: The Clue in the Secret Passage
The Shoebox Kids: The Broken Dozen Mystery
The Shoebox Kids: The Case of the Secret Code

To the Last Man (Pacific Press: Publishers)

WITH CÉLESTE PERRINO WALKER

Digital and Print:
Salome's Charger (Foundation Series Book #1)

Printed in Great Britain
by Amazon